# THE GUARDIANS

*A True Tale of Travels in the Arizona Territory*

Ernie Stech

Order this book online at www.trafford.com
or email orders@trafford.com

Most Trafford titles are also available at major online book retailers.

Printed in the United States of America.

ISBN: 978-1-4269-3528-2 (sc)

ISBN: 978-1-4269-3529-9 (hc)

ISBN: 978-1-4269-3530-5 (e-book)

Library of Congress Control Number: 2010908506

*Our mission is to efficiently provide the world's finest, most comprehensive book publishing
service, enabling every author to experience success. To find out how to publish your book, your
way, and have it available worldwide, visit us online at www.trafford.com*

*Trafford rev. 6/2/2010*

 www.trafford.com

**North America & international**
toll-free: 1 888 232 4444 (USA & Canada)
phone: 250 383 6864 ♦ fax: 812 355 4082

*For Hilary, Lisa, Bill, and Preston and also PJ, Emma, Chelsea, Brad, and Samantha who know how strange and interesting your father and grandfather can be.*

# *Editor's Note*

**I have traveled through southeastern** Utah numerous times from my home in Flagstaff, Arizona. The route involves taking US Highway 89 north out of Flagstaff up to the intersection with US Route 160 and then to Tuba City and Kayenta on the Navajo Reservation. At Kayenta the traveler has a choice of continuing on 160 over to Teec Nos Pos, Arizona and from that point to Farmington, New Mexico or Cortez, Arizona. The other option is to make a left turn at Kayenta and proceed through Monument Valley, still on the Navajo Reservation, into Utah, across the San Juan river at Mexican Hat, and then to Bluff and Blanding both small towns and mostly Mormon. Beyond Blanding is Monticello and then Moab and slickrock country, now a favorite of mountain bike enthusiasts.

During one such trip to Utah I stopped in Bluff for lunch at a combination restaurant and gift store. After a lunch consisting of a Navajo taco and a diet soda, I got back into my car and started to drive away when I saw a sign in front of one of the nearby houses announcing a yard sale. Normally I do not go to yard sales, but I was running well ahead of schedule and needed to take a somewhat longer break from driving after a steady three and a half hours on the road.

The yard sale presented the usual assortment of odds and ends that might be acquired or found around a home in a small town. I looked over some of the items and talked briefly with the youngish woman who presided over the sale. It turned out that she and her husband had purchased the house six months earlier and were cleaning out all the stuff that had been left behind.

The only item that caught my attention was an old portable writing desk, the original and low tech laptop writing device. It was about twenty inches wide and twelve inches deep with a slanted top surface. That top was the cover of a simple wooden box about four inches thick. It was hinged and held down with a rusty hasp and eye. The hinges were leather and in bad shape, dry and flaking.

At a price of two dollars I could not resist buying the writing desk with the thought that I might be able to resuscitate it and actually use it at times for my own writing. The artifact went into the trunk of my car and was forgotten until I got back to Flagstaff a week later. At the point I removed it and left it in my garage. It was not until three months later, in a slack time in my writing career, that I noticed the writing desk again and operated on it. That involved prying the hasp loose and trying to rotate the lid. No such luck. The whole thing came up and off in my hands, the leather hinges having long since lost any flexibility.

Inside the writing desk was a sheaf of papers. They appeared to be an early form of writing tablet, lined and similar to a legal pad. However the sheets were all loose and aged even though they had not been exposed to sunlight. There were about a hundred sheets of paper covered with careful, clear, and small handwriting in the traditional loopy Spencerian script.

Leaving the portable writing desk, now in two pieces, in the garage, I took the sheets of paper into the house and began to read. According to the first page everything that followed was the recorded story of one Pietr Raul O'Leary who had traveled through northern Arizona and southern Utah at some time in the past. There was no information on who had transcribed the story after listening to O'Leary. Whoever it was had done a good job of recording not only the story but the language of the teller. .

Some research I did later that year in the area extending from Mexican Hat through Bluff to Blanding, Utah indicated that a Pietr Raul O'Leary did not live in the area. At least there was no record of him ever living anywhere from Mexican Hat northward. There is no record of his having died and been buried in that part of the state of Utah either.

His story is presented here as neither a valid record of the state of affairs in what is now known as Monument Valley when he visited the area nor as pure fiction. It may be that O'Leary suffered from hallucinations or enjoyed a vivid fantasy life. At any rate, if there really was an O'Leary, he apparently did not intend to profit from the telling since the record existed in the form of the bundle of tablet sheets described above. It is possible that O'Leary's story was a work of fiction by some anonymous writer in an earlier time, perhaps of Mormon settlement.

I have transcribed the handwritten material and attempted to organize it to some extent. I have also felt it necessary to interpolate comments throughout the work because some of O'Leary's statements are hard to accept. For example, he refers to the "Moqui" who inhabited Monument Valley when he traveled through. "Moqui" is an old and disrespectful name for the Hopi residents of Arizona, and I am not sure that they ever lived in Monument Valley. In addition, Monument Valley at the time O'Leary was likely to have traveled there was populated not by Hopi but by Navajo.

# *Testimony*

**This is the true story** of my time in the north part of the Arizona Territory as I told it to a person who wrote it down. I have set my mark below to show that this is the true story. 'Cause I cannot read, I had some people read to me the story as it was set down, and what I heard was pretty much the truth as I told it. You can believe it or not. Makes no difference to me.

**Pietr Raul O'Leary**

# How I Come to the Big Black Rock

**I was workin' my way** up north to the San Juan River that fall. I had come up the river they call the Small Colorado, at least I think that was it. Anyway, I left it behind at a tradin' post and headed almost straight north. There was a big dark mesa along to my right as I worked my way up. Near the end of that mesa I seen a arroyo or as you would call it a small canyon that had some water in it. The water was in pools. So I went down into it so's I could have somethin' to drink ever once in a while as I worked my way up north. Eventual I came up to kind of the end of that arroyo or canyon as you would call it but it was really small up at the north end and not really a canyon at all. While I was in the arroyo I seen one of them tarantula spiders which is good for scarin' girls and young women but really ain't dangerous at all, and I heard rattles from them rattlesnakes two times but never seen those critters.

As I come up out of it I seen a tall black rock stickin' up out of the ground. I have drawed a picture of it for you to see. It looked like something God hisself had hurled itdown into the ground. Kind of like a real big arrowhead with the back end stuck in the ground. I mean really big because it stood what seemed like a couple hundred feet high. I was glad to see that thing because it was the landmark they had told me about down south earlier in the spring. I knew I was on the right track to get to the San Juan if I seen that big black rock stickin' up there.

This here part of the country is real dry in September when I was walkin' through it. They usual have summer rain storms but they had left early the year I was there so it was real dusty. Ever step I took raised some little cloud of dust, and my boots, which is real old and worn, was covered with the red and brown dust. All the time I seen ravens floatin' around over my head, but they is everywhere in the Arizona Territory and particular up in this north part.

So I walked over to the big black rock after fillin' both my canteens from the couple pools of water in the bottom of the arroyo. I been told that it quite a ways yet to the San Juan from there and maybe there wouldn't be any water along the way. If there was it would be at the bottom of the river. Anyway, I come close to that big black rock and seen a person up ahead. At least I thought it was a person. It was kinda small and hunched over. I hadn't seen anyone in awhile so I walked over toward it. What I seen was somewhat scary even to someone like me who has seen a lot in his many years out in the woods and desert.

It was a man. A human man. I could see that. But he wasn't like any man I had ever seen afore. He didn't look like no Navaho or Moqui Indian. I seen a lot of them back to the south. This man was kinda small and shriveled up. He didn't look like no Chinee either. I seen some of

2

them back in San Francisco when I shipped out one time. He wasn't no Negro man either. Them I seen down in other parts of Arizona after the War Between the States, that's the way I was taught to say it by some teacher lady. They was part of the Buffalo Soldiers Brigade. Or somethin' like that.

I sure didn't like the looks of this little shriveled up man. He looked like one of them Egypt mummy people. Except he was standing up. And he was real dark suntanned. Or else had real dark skin. Never saw a living standing mummy before. Don't every hope to see one again.

I kinda stood back to see what he would do. He didn't do nothin'. Just stood there. I wans't really scared 'cause I had been around a lot and seen a lot of strange things in my day. Strange people, too. One time I seen a two headed lady in one of them carnival places. I also seen two people hooked together at their heads at another one of them carnivals.

Here I gotta stop and tell you somethin'. The people what knew I was comin' up this way told me about the big black rock. They told about another one up farther north and a little to the west that you couldn't see yet but it was there. And there was one other one way over to the east. I could also see a small black rock maybe a couple miles away from the big black one. Anyway, those black rocks made kind of a triangle. Except that the two rocks near where I was made kind of a short other side to the triangle. So the thing would have looked something like this if you drawed it on the ground. Or even on a piece of paper. Which I did not have.

Way east rock (which I couldn't see.)

Northwest Rock (which I couldn't see)

Other Smaller Rock

Rock where I was.

*Editor's Note: This "triangle" seems to have consisted of what is now Mount Agathla near Kayenta, Arizona as "Rock Where I Was" and Shiprock was "Way East Rock." The "Northwest Rock" probably is Alhambra Rock located near Mexican Hat, Utah. The "Other Smaller Rock" was probably what is now known at Church Rock also near Kayenta. All of these landmarks are readily visible in driving around the area and are identified on topographic maps.*

So there was that triangle thing. The shortest way to the San Juan was kinda through that triangle thing. In between was a bunch of red rock buttes. They was real big. Some had rock spikes standing up. I mean rock spikes. A couple that I seen later were nothing but those spike things sticking up. It was interestin'. I wished I had drawed them when I was there but didn't have no paper.

So anyway, I stand about ten yards away from this little scrawny man and he don't say nothin'. He don't nod or nothin'. Just kinda looks at me and then looks at the ground. He never looks up. Never looks up at the big black rock that is right aside him.

Seems like he didn't want me to go any futher.

Now lookin' back, I shoulda just took more notice and gone around the long way to the San Juan. But me, I was in a hurry, and I didn't see no reason to go any but the straight way. Which I did. Later I wished I hadn't.

# How I Went Past the Big Black Rock and Met Up with a Dust Devil

**Well I wasn't gonna let** no little dwarf stop me from goin' on to the San Juan the straightest way I knew. So I walked right past that little dwarf man. He wasn't really dwarf, I just like to call him that 'cause it makes me feel good. Actual he was prob'ly five foot four or so. Not much shorter than me.

Anyway I walked right past him and didn't pay no attention to him. Then I walked right up to that big black rock and started around it. I turned about and looked back and then was when I got kinda a little scared 'cause that little man was lookin' right at me real strange. I thought maybe I should turn back and go some other way. But the San Juan was sure callin' to me.

It was futher around that big black rock than I thought. The dang thing was higher up than I thought too. It stood up at least five hundred – maybe six hundred – feet. It sure went straight up, too. Not a rock that you would want to climb.

So I walked on around it lookin' back ever once in a while and that little man kept kinda trackin' me. Lookin' at me. He stayed a good ways back. Like he didn't want to get too close to me 'cause maybe I was dangerous or somethin'. my pistol, too.

I went past that big black rock about a mile when I seen one of them dust devils spout up ahead. If you ain't never seen one, they is strange. Looks like a little typhoon or one of them tornadoes except the dust devil is a lot smaller. It twists and turns just like a typhoon or tornado but it's all dust. No rain or nothin' like that. They springs up ever once in a while in the desert or real dry country. I seen them in all kinds a places in Arizona and futher west. They's usually seen in the summer when's hot.

So this dust devil just scoots up outa the sand and dirt in front of me. I didn't pay it much mind. They's a lot of them things around as I said before. But this one started comin' right at me which was real strange. Usually they just kinda wander around and then wrap theirselves up into the sky. I guess the get so tight wound that they wrap theirselves around theirselves and disappear. Or somethin' like that.

Well this one didn't do none of that. It just marched right at me. I never seen that before so I stopped and watched it. Danged if it didn't just keep comin' in a straight line right at me. That's when I got a little worried. Never knowed whether one of them things might fling you up in the air. I didn't want that to happen. But there was no where to run. So I stood there until it got right close. That's when I figured I had to do somethin'. So I hunkered down a bit, kinda sat on my heels. Put my hands down on the sand.

Well danged if that thing didn't come right at me. Next thing I knew I was in the middle of that dust devil. That's kinda the last thing I remember. At least for a while. When I come back to my senses, it seemed like my brains was all muddled. Everythin' was real confused. I kinda turned and didn't see any dust devil anymore. But it sure did somethin' to my brains, as I said before.

I couldn't think worth a tinker's damn. Was like I didn't have any ideas at all. Wasn't just jumbled. Was like that dust devil had sucked all the ideas out of my head. Fact I touched the top of my head to make sure there wasn't no hole in it.

So I was half sittin' there about a mile from that big black rock with my brains all muddled up. First time that ever happen to me. I mean I been somewhat affected by whiskey at times. But that was way different. When you drink too much whiskey you kinda know what you has done. You can still sorta think. But this was way different from that.

I also smoked some kinda weed with a Indian friend down in south Arizona. That was real interestin'. Made you feel real good. Made you feel like to really didn't want to do nothin' for a while. Which I didn't do.

But you still knew you had token the stuff. You figured it would wear off and you would want to do things again. All the time you was still kinda thinkin'.

That whiskey and that weed was both real different from what I was feelin' out there in sight of that big black rock. I just couldn'a thunk at all.

# *That's When Those Women Come Up to Me*

**Next thing I know there** is seven women standing around me and that little ol' guy what I passed some time afore. They was all lookin' at me. An' I'm sittin' there on the ground with my brains all muddled up not knowing what was happenin'. One of them women starts talkin' to me in a language I never heard afore. 'Course there's lotsa languages I never heard before. But this didn't sound like no Navajo language. And it sure as heck wasn't no Spanish 'cause I heard many a word in Spanish. I do know this woman was not talkin' sweet talk to me. No sir! She seemed real upset. Then she would talk to the little ol' guy.

First she's pointin' up at that big black rock and then at me. She's real upset from what I could see and understand. It was mostly how kinda loud she was talkin'. And there was a lot of finger pointin' and arm wavin'. Them other women was standin' there listenin' and for the most part they was noddin' their heads just like White folk do. I ain't never seen a real Indian nod his head. I mean by real Indian one of them that's not been around White folk. Mostly them Indians look kinda blank even when they is mad or when they is happy. The would make right good poker players although I never played much poker 'cause I never had much money and didn't want to lose what I had. Me I also never did drink much cause it made me sick and give me watery eyes. I had to keep my mind swift and my eyes clear 'cause I spent most of my time out of doors in the deserts and forests, and

11

you can't live long there with your eyes al bleary and your mind muddled up with drink. But I guess that's not real important to this story.

Well I was still layin' there on the ground when two of them women come over and had me sit up straight. I woulda just as soon kept layin' down, but they just picked me up and set me down like I was a little old jackrabbit or somethin'. Once I was settin' there I could see them women more better. They all looked pretty darn strong. And I wouldn'a called any of 'em real pretty. They was just your average Indian woman. They was maybe in the thirties, but you can't always tell with Indian women 'cause they is outdoors a lot and work a lot so's their skin gets kinda wrinkled and old lookin' even when they is young. Sometimes I think them Indian women work harder and longer than the men do. Men seem to spend a lot of their time smokin' and sittin' around talkin' about what they done or what they're gonna do. I guess they do go huntin' sometimes. Them men also got to dig in the fields and plant the corn and beans and stuff. At least them what's into farmin' and gardenin'. But that kinda work don't take too long. I mean it just happens every once in a while. Them women are workin' all the time. Grindin' corn. Cookin' meals. Tendin' to the kids. And they got to make their clothes out of deerskins and such 'though where they find dear out there in the desert I do not know.

Anyways them women now come closer to me. I guess they wanted a closer look at this old coot. When I ain't really a old coot. I just look older 'cause I'm like them Indians. Spend a lot of time out of doors and in the sun. I mean my skin ain't no peaches and cream like some of the ads I seen for women's skin ointments in store windows. Best stuff I ever got for my skin was some udder cream from a dairy farmer back in Illinois. Trouble is there ain't no dairy farmers in the Arizona Territory.

Anyway I thought them women was gonna poke me to see if I was real. But they didn't. They just did a lot of lookin'. Real close, too. One of them actual came up right in front of my face and looked all up and down my face until I was getting' nervous. A couple of them looked over my hair which is real scraggly. By the time all this happened I had not had a haircut in some three months and the last time I washed my hair it was mostly with sand and a little water down by the Little Colorado River, if that is what it was. So I figured that maybe they was goin' to scalp me or somethin' like that. But I knowed that these Arizona Territory Indians never did much scalpin'. That was most Indians in other parts of the United States of America. I never been to any of them parts.

They sure thought I was a interestin' specimen. It was like they had never seen a White man before which I could not believe. There musta been White men come through here before 'cause I was s'posed to meet some of them up beyond the San Juan River. Anyway all this lookin' and inspectin' went on for what seemed like a real long time. Long enough that now I was wantin' to get up, you know, stand up, but I figured that might not set too well with them women, and they outnumbered me by quite a bit.

That's when the little ol' man come up from somewhere and pointed at me. I didn't know what was the meanin' of that.

# How They Hogtied Me
# and Rode Me Up a Butte

**Well next thing I know** they got me hogtied. By that I mean they tied my legs down at the ankles and right around my wrists on my arms. Now then they pushed a pole atween my ankles and my wrists and lifted me up off the ground. I tell you that was a mighty painin' to be lifted up like that. No sooner had they lifted me up than they started walkin' with me. All I could see was two o' them women up front holdin' up the pole with their hands and I guessed there was two more behind me. They wasn't real gentle with me, I can tell you. I bounced up and down and started grittin' my teeth 'cause it was right painin'.

After a while I found out I could kinda lift myself up a bit and move the legs and arms so's at least the painin' was in different parts of them legs and arms. That kinda helped but it was still not so good. The other thing was that this was not a real dignified way to be taken somewhere slung up on a pole like a damn pig bein' taken to a roast or some such. So my dignity – such as I had – was painin' as much as my arms and legs.

O' course it didn't help none that they was four women carrying me along like that. So I couldna felt any lower. Shoulda just walked some other way than right at the big black rock. But I ain't never been known to take the long way when there was a short way!

Now it was still afternoon when all this was happenin'. Up ahead I seen a big red butte. I could kinda turn my head a little and that's how I seen that butte. Later on I seen all kinds of them red buttes there in that land. Nobody ever told me about them when they was tellin' how to get to the San Juan River.

*Editor's Note: The "big red butte" that O'Leary describes here was one of the many small mesas in what is now Monument Valley. It is these red mesas that give Monument Valley its name. There is no real distinction between "butte" and "mesa" today. It may have been that smaller mesas, standing alone, were at one time referred to as buttes.*

Next thing I know they set me down and seems like four other women picked me up after a little bit. They wasn't no gentler that the first four. Well they head right for the first big red butte. Then sure as can be they walk right up to that butte, and I see a kinda trail up the side of the damn thing! I'm thinkin' to myself that we sure as hell can't be goin' up there. But that's what they did. Somehow they built thereselves a trail right up the side of that butte! I couldn't believe it. It was real narrow. I thought it was too narrow for two people to walk side by alongside each other. What they did, I saw, was the two women in front were walkin' one in front of the other each of them still holdin' the damn pole in their hands. I said to myself: 'Thank goodness they're not holdin' the damn pole on their shoulders. I sure as hell would be fallin' off that trail and be done for. Forever.'

Once we got on top of that butte, they set me down and let me walk on my own. But they didn't give me much room! I mean they kept crowded around me kinda like a posse would if you was about to be hanged.

I could see a long ways from on top of that butte. An' I tried to see as much as I could 'cause I was thinkin' about how to get out of there and travel on to the San Juan. Only problem was I couldn't figure how to get down off that thing! It sure was a long ways down, and I didn't see no stairs!

# *What They Did Up on That Butte*

**By the time we got** to the top of that butte it was close to sunsettin' time. I didn't what to expect, but I found out soon enough. Them women was still around me and that ol' guy what I seen when I first come up to the big black rock. They untied me after settin' the pole down. And my wrists and ankles was still hurtin' from that ride they gave me. It musta taken at least a hour or two to get to the butte and then up it.

Well next thing I know there is a lot more people. I seen them coming over the edge of that butte right where the trail was so the word musta spread that they had found theirselves some kinda human critter or somethin'. Ever one of them come over to look at me where I was layin' on the ground. Now I wasn't goin' to get up or nothin' with all of them there. They could darn well sit me up or stand me up but I wasn't goin' to do it on my own.

After a whole bunch of them had got up there on the butte I seen a ol' man come up over the edge of the butte, and he was not the same as the little man over by the Big Black Rock. Ever one gave way in front of him so I figured he must be a chief or medicine man or some such. I met him somewhat later as I will tell you when we come to it. He come over and looked at me. I mean he looked right at me, right in the eyeballs. And I looked him right back! I wasn't goin' to be scared by no one here. If they was goin' to kill me and eat me or some such then they could go right ahead. I hoped they knowed that I wasn't goin' to taste no good. I mean

I was a real skinny kinda man. Eatin' me woulda been like chewin' on a old piece of jerky. And I mean old. A piece that was so dried out it woulda looked like a piece of wood! The wouldn'a had to dry my meat. I was about as dry as any jerky you could find anywheres! And there wouldn'a been that much of me. I guess I probably weighed about a hunnert and twenty at my fattest, and that ain't very fat!

Well this old guy looks at me for a while, and I looks back at him. The he nods his head, and I figured that was the end of me. But I was wrong. Everbody kinda stood back from me. They made up a circle. First they was all facin' in towards me. Then they all turned about and faced away. They waited some time. Then them folks started a kinda shuffle dance. If you seen Indian dances that's the way they do. They don't do that fancy steppin' that you see among White folk. Nope they just kinda shuffle their feet. I hear a drum that someone musta brought up on the butte. So they do that shuffle dance for a while and then they stop. I guess they wanted to rest or some such.

By this time the sun is set but it still ain't dark. If you ever was out in the Arizona Territories you would know that the light lasts a long time after the sun goes over the edge. Well that's the way it was when they started dancin' again. But this time they come over to me, one at a time, and look at my face. Each one of them done that. I figured that was part of the way they would see which part of me they was gonna eat! Then they stopped and rested again.

I was getting' a little tired of all this dancin' with no other action. But there wasn't nothin' I could do so I just lay there on the ground, and I could start to see the stars in the sky over to the east where the sun was long gone. There was just about a half moon comin' up in the east.

Then they start dancin' again. This time they come over one at a time, and they kinda poke me. I guess they wanted to find out how meaty I was! It was like they was testin' the meat before the meal. That was okay. By now I was sure they was gonna butcher me and have me for their supper. I just hoped they would whack me on the head real good before they started cuttin' off the parts they wanted.

But I was wrong. After all that dancin' and lookin' and pokin' they just sit me up and make some kinda gesture. I guess they wanted me to stand up. So I did. It feel real good. By then it was fair to middlin' dark. That was the end of the time on top of the butte. I wasn't gonna be nobody's supper that night.

# They Put Me in a Little Dark Room

**Well then they walked me** back down from that butte in the night, and I couldn't see nothin'. It was mostly men what walked me down there kinda single file with some in front and some in back. There wasn't no women when we went down. I don't know how they got down. Or when they got down. Somehow these men guided me down that trail. I coulda fell off anytime, but they was careful with me. At least they didn't hogtie me again and hoist me onto that pole.

At the bottom of the butte there was a bunch of little Indian houses that I could barely see 'cause there weren't no fire except one and it was kept real small. Right as we got down there was a hut with a fence around it, one of them wooden fences the Indians make. Kinda like one of our split rail fences. But it was high. It was higher than my head. As we come down I could kinda see into the place behind the fence but when we got down I couldn't see nothin' in there. And that is where they put me. Inside that fence and inside that little hut. I mean there wasn't nothin' in there. One of them Indians threw my bedroll in and then they closed the door. That's the last I seen of them for quite a time. Not sure how long a time 'cause, as I will tell you, they kept me in that hut for quite a time.

I was kinda tired after all the being hauled up the butte and then walked back down so I unrolled my bedroll and laid down on it. The floor was just plain dirt but I have slept on dirt much of my life so's that didn't bother me in any way. Pretty soon I guess I was asleep. Didn't woken up for sometime. When I did I could see light between some of the cracks in the walls. I tried to open the door but it wouldn't budge. I pushed and pulled on that thing and it wouldn't move either way. So I was stuck in this little hut.

Now I was getting' hungry havin' not eaten since a day before. And I sure coulda used some water. But all I could do was sit there and wonder what was goin' to happen to me. Figured I had ventured into some real bad place. Without knowin' what I was doin'. It sure didn't feel no good sitiin' in that little shack with no one else around. I couldn't even hear nothin'. It was like I was dead or somethin'.

Then sometime that mornin' someone came to my little shack and shoved a pot of water through a hole in the door. Now it was one of them Indian pots. You know made out of clay. This one was pretty good size. Did I ever drink outta that pot. Water tasted old and musty but I wouldn't waste any or turn it down.

Then the hut started to heat up 'cause it was still September in the Arizona Territories. That sun still got up there pretty high. I could see the light through the cracks in the walls. Some light made lines of light on the floor so's I could kinda follow where the sun was going. Near as I could figure the door to the hut faced east.

That hut was pretty small. It was 'bout ten feet by ten feet. I figure that 'cause I am 'bout five foot two and I could almost lay myself twice over from wall to wall. The room was just short of ten foot four.

I could hear some of them Indian folks talkin' sometimes but not very clear. Now my hearin's pretty good from a lot of practice in trackin' animals and people but I sure couldn't make out their voices very good. Whatever it was they was talkin's it was not English or anythin' like it. It sounded real strange to me. A little like some of the Moqui talk I heard once or twice while travelin' through their territory. Them Moqui was generally pretty easy to get along with. Most of them would invite you in and even feed you. They didn't talk a lot. Wouldn't answer most questions. Even the ones what could speak English. All I could say in their language was 'thank you.' I learnt that from one of them that was pretty good about speaking English. At least he could get his ideas across. As long as you was interested in farmin' and food and huntin'. 'Course that's all I was interested in anyway. Coulda cared less about their ways and what they did in their kivas. Heck I don't particularly care what goes in most churches when I been in towns. I figure that if I act good towards most people and don't do too much harm then I will get all right after I die. Some Hindu guy got ahold of me one time and told me all about how when you die you come back as some other kind of being, like a dog or horse or mountain lion. I listened okay to him but didn't believe what he said. Ever'body got their own way of thinkin' about dying and what happens after. I don't spend a lot of time thinkin' about it. Never had much time. Had to spend most of my time just getting' food and water and stayin' alive.

Now it was kinda dark in that little hut most of the day even with the little bits of sun comin' through the cracks. And I was still kinda hungry. Then about what seemed like in the afternoon someone pushed one of them clay bowls through the door. I went over and picked it up. It smelled like food when I held it up to my nose. So I stuck my fingers in it and tasted the stuff. It was some kinda corn mush or somethin' like that. It sure tasted good to me.

I'm not a real big fella. As I said, I'm only five foot two. And real skinny. That's 'cause I walk a lot and don't eat so much. If any of them cannonbals that eat's people would try me he would find I'd be real chewy and not very tasty. No, I would not make a very good meal. No part of me. My leg's is real thin and tough. Even those big upper leg parts. I figure I'm prob'ly human jerky on the hoof! Ha, ha!

So I was tryin' to figure out what they was goin' to do with me. I wasn't' goin' to be no good meal for anyone. 'Sides I didn't think they was human eaters anyway. Didn't act like they were. And I never heard of no cannonbals in this part of the Arizona Territory. If they asked me, I woulda said "Just let me go on to the San Juan River 'cause I don't mean to do anyone here any harm." But m'am, they didn't ask!

*Editor's note: This is the first of several indications that the person recording and transcribing the story was a woman.*

Not much I could do but set there and then lay down and then set up again and sometimes walk around a little in that hut. 'Course there wasn't much room to walk and it got kina hot in there. At least I wasn't hungry after that bowl of corn mush. I scraped out every last bit of that mush from that bowl. Then I even licked it clean. Figured I didn't know how much longer I was goin' to be in there. Then I had this thought that maybe they was tryin' to fatten me up what with no walkin' and some real nourishin' food like that corn mush.

I put the bowl by the door and sure 'nough someone come along, reached in, and pulled it out. That's when I laid down by that little place in the door where they put the food through and tried to look out. Didn't do no good. All I could see was the lower part of the fence around the place. Wasn't anybody there. If I did seem a body it woulda been their feet and maybe ankles. I just couldn't get my eyeballs far enough down to look up. So it seems as if I was more or less stuck in that little hut until these Indian folk decided to let me out.!

Now it was normal real dark in that little hut, but there was them slits in the walls that let some light in. That was for one day. Next day when it was light out I heard these folks on the outside talkin' a bit in their strange language and kinda putterin' around. Well next thing I know they is caulkin' up them little slits! It gets darker and darker in that little hut 'til I could barely see anythin' at all. So I set in the dark for the rest of that day and couldn't keep track of what time of day it was or even what day it was. They was all muddled together.

This was real strange to me 'cause I had spent most of my life, as I have said before, out in the open. In the desert and in the mountains. Even in the mountains with their forests there was always light, and you could always tell what time of day it was. At least you could tell if it was day or night. I couldn't do that no more!

I was right upset by this new situation. So I tried to shake them walls and see if I could knock some of the caulking out but that didn't work. I was just kinda stuck in this dark place. I don't know, ma'm, how long I was in there, but I tell you it was not a nice time in my life.

After some time I thought maybe I had died. I wasn't me anymore. I mean I wasn't killed earthly dead 'cause I was still breathin' and gettin' hungry and such. So it seemed like I wasn't me anymore, but I wasn't someone else either. You know, ma'm, I wasn't me or someone else, and that's real bothersome. Everybody ought to be somebody. Here I was being nothin'.

I never been that way before. Maybe when I was borned to my sweet Mama I was a nobody, but then I become somebody pretty fast. I knowed I was somebody as far back as I can remember which is back to when my Daddy whupped me for somethin' I did. Can't remember what I did but remember the whuppin'.

Then that little door for the food opened, and there was a little light. The food bowl come through the little door which was then shut. I quick like went over and tried to push the little door open but it was stuck shut. All I could do was feel around for that bowl of corn mush. I ate it with my fingers, and it sure tasted good. But I didn't feel so good.

Eventual I got tired and went to sleep. Never knew how hard it was to sleep in the complete dark! I kept hearin' sounds. When you can't see nothin' but you hear things, that'll spook you. At least it spooked me. So

I slept fitful that night. I guess it was night. It coulda been that day. I did not know. But I sure did care!

Well that bigger door finally opened, and it was early in the mornin'. I knew that because the sun was comin' up in front of the little hut with its door facin' east. The little ol' man I seen at the big black rock was standin' there at the door. He moved his hand like he wanted me to come out which I did. Then he kinda lead me out of the yard around that little hut and out into the open of that Indian village.

# *How They Kept Me Up Two Nights with No Sleep*

**The next thing that happened** was just about as strange as anythin' up to that time but not as strange as some of the stuff that would happen later. What looked like the whole tribe was standing there looking at the old man and me. He held up his right hand and started talking to the people. They all just stood there and didn't nod their heads or nothin'. Just listened to the old man. Now he talked on for some time, and I was getting' kinda muddled in my head standin' in the sun like that after what was prob'ly a couple of days in that dark hut. Finally the old man stopped talkin' and turns around to look at me. I guess he seen that I weren't doin' too well, so he has me set down right where I am. That made me feel a bit better.

While I'm sittin' there he starts talkin' to me. Well more like talkin' and at the same time gesturin' with his hands and arms 'cause he knows I can't understand a word of his language. I know he slows down his talkin' from when he was talkin' to his own folk. While I'm about ready to scratch my head as we White folk do when we is all muddled up in the head.

I guess he figures out this ain't makin' no sense to me so he stops. For a minute I think he is goin' to scratch his head 'cause he looks real muddled up too. Like his brain is as muddled as mine. But I know it ain't. Finally he comes over and sets down right in front of me which I think its fine 'cause it's easier than lookin' up at him.

So he sets there for a coupla minutes before doin' anythin'. The he looks me right in the eye. Next thing is he shuts his eyes, leans his head over like he's pretendin' to sleep. Then he looks at me and does it again. I nod and try to show that I understand he's tellin' me about sleep. I make a couple of dumb gestures that I hope show I understand. So he does the same thing over, shows me about sleep but this time he shakes his head sideways, makes a slashin' sign across his throat, and then takes both hands, puts them together, and slides them out sideways all of them bein', I think, ways to tell me "No." I musta still looked muddled 'cause he did it again. Then I understand what he is sayin': no sleep!

Well didn't that beat nothin'! Here I just got done layin' around and sleepin' in that little hut and now he says "No sleep." 'Course at first I didn't understand he was meanin' me. Then I seen that he was pointing at me and again makin' all them signs about no sleep. So I guessed he was wantin' me to somehow not have any sleep for a while. That was okay by me 'cause I was kinda slept out at that time.

Now he starts drawin' a picture in the dirt in front of me. It is a map of my little hut and the fence around it. He turns around and points at the fence and the little hut inside. I nod 'cause that's all I could think of doin'. I guess he understood my nod 'cause he nodded back. Then he points at me and points at the yard and the little hut. So I get the idea that he wants me to go back into the yard and little hut. I start to get up but he stops me by showin' me with both his hands to sit down again. He kinda moves his hands down to the ground. So I sit.

Next thing I know he is drawin' more pictures in the sand. He draws a picture of the sun. I knowed that 'cause he drawed a round thing with rays comin' out of it. I knowed that was the Indian sign for the sun. Then right next to it he draws a picture of the moon. I knowed that 'cause it was one of them little curvy moons and not a whole complete circle. Well I sure don't know what is goin' on here. Then he does that all over again, a sun and a moon. Finally he draws a line between the first moon and the next sun. Well I figure that amounts to two days. I nod and hold up two fingers, and the old man nods back.

Then he points to the two days and once again signs me no sleep. Well damn, excuse me ma'm but damn he wants me to stay awake for two days and two nights. This is a whole strange place that I am in, and these Indians are a whole strange kind. But what was I to do? They had me by the shirttails, and there was no way for me to do anythin' but what they asked. So I shrug my shoulders, which probably means nothin' to him, and nod my head. What the heck, if they want me to stay up for two days and two nights, I can do that. I've been asked to do worse, I guess, but I couldn't think of what or where right at that time.

So the old man gets up, and I get up, too. He walks me back to my little hut and the yard around it and leaves me there. Then a couple o' them Indian women come in and bring me a heap of food. I mean like it was some of their flat bread, some corn mush, some nuts of some kind I couldn't right off recognize, and dried squash. The squash had been cut into strips and dried. They quick like showed me how to put the squash into a bowl with water and make it so it was able to be eaten. And then they brung me three great jugs of water. Those jugs was like to hold three-four gallons of water each. So I was pretty well fixed for food and water.

That's when I heard the rest of them Indians, at least some of 'em, startin' to do a dance and the kind of chantin'-singin' they do along with the beat of a drum. Everybody leaves my little hut and yard, and they close the door to the fence and I am left all alone in there for two days, I guess, with no sleep. Now I didn't know how they was going to keep me from sleeping, but I figured I could do some quick sleepin' ever once in a while. Well I was wrong about that.

Them Indians kept up that chantin' and drummin' for two days and two nights 'til it like to have drove me crazy! They stopped ever once in a while. Just about as I was to fall asleep they would start up again.

Well you talk about one muddled brain. Mine was total muddled after the first half day, and it wasn't even dark out yet! I didn't have any real troubles until what I figured was after midnight of the first night. It was real dark out there being no moon at all. It musta set sometime earlier than night. I didn't notice. There was a lot of stars but other than that it was total dark.

That's when it started. I mean my muddled brain just started makin' up things. First I seen my Mama comin' at me in the yard, and she was real as could be. 'O course she weren't really there. Every time I tried to reach out to her she would kinda melt away. Then she would come back again. She never looked at me. Never smiled or nothin'. Just kinda stood there in the yard. One time I noticed she weren't exactly standin' on the ground. She was lifted up about a foot or so above the ground. That's when I knew I was goin'.

Next thing I noticed that night, after Mama left, was that I could hear my own heart beatin' in my chest, and it was beatin' in the same way as them Indian drums. This kinda scared me 'cause I had never actual heard my heart beatin' away like that. It got to soundin' louder and louder 'til I thought it might just jump right out of me. But it didn't. There was other things that happened that night that I can't remember anymore.

Then the sun come up on the second day and it was the usual big bright September sun that you could expect in that part of the Arizona Territory. By this time I was real sleepy but 'tween the sun and that darn drummin' and chantin' there was no way I could sleep. I tried goin' in the hut and laid down but just could not, in any way, fall asleep. So then I went outside and sat there for a while until the sun got a little too hot for me, and then I went around to the side of my little hut and sat in the shade. Them Indians just kept up their chantin' and drummin' it seemed like every half hour or so.

I fixed myself a kinda meal if you can call some flat bread, corn mush, and a cup of water a meal. I also soaked some o' them squash strips in my cup and chewed on 'em. Wasn't too tasty but better than anythin' else I had around.

After my lunch my brain is so muddled that I think that maybe I am not where I think I am but somewhere else but then couldn't figure out where else I could be. I didn't feel like I was there anymore but kinda floatin' around. Then I thought maybe I had died and this was my soul floatin' around lookin' at things. I even thought I could see them Indians doin' their chantin' and drummin' even though they was outside of the fence around my yard. My soul or whatever it was went even higher in the sky until I could see the whole Indian village and the buttes around it. I think someday folks will figure out how to fly like birds and then they will be able to see things that way. I mean from way up high. I couldn't get so high as to see the whole of the Arizona Territory, though. That was way too big.

I end up floatin' around like that for a long time. Sometime I even seen things that I remembered from my travels in the mountains and deserts, but I could see it all from above which was real strange. Ended up so's I kinda had fun floatin' around like that but then it was all over and I was sittin' in the shade next to my little hut.

By this time I needed some more food so I made the same meal of flat bread, corn mush, softened up squash strips, and a few cups of water. That made me real sleepy, all that food. So I laid my head back against the wall of the little hut and was just about to fall asleep when there is this great hollerin' and screamin' from them Indians. That sure woke me up. It sounded like they had just been attacked by the U. S. cavalry and was ready to go to war. They musta knowed that I was about to fall asleep. Maybe they peeked over the fence or some such. Anyway, I sure woken up and stayed woken up for a good time after all the noise.

About this time I noticed somethin' real peculiar. The drummin' and chantin' was still goin' on, but it seemed like it was just a part of the world like anything else. You know like birds singin' or the wind whippin' through trees or any other natural sound. It was like them sounds had always been there, and I had heard them all my life!

The thing that happened next muddled my brain even more. I was sittin' there in the yard around my little hut in the night time with the stars shinin' real pretty. This was in the night time of the second day. I was just sittin' there with my brain kinda blank when I started seein' some creatures. They was human bein's but of a real strange kind. They all just stood around and didn't do much of anythin'. At first they was kinda fuzzy like you was lookin' at 'em through a fog or some such. The longer I seen them in my brain the more clear they become. That's when I seen that they was all real white and real skinny and their faces was all drawn back so's they almost looked like a head skull with skin kinda stretched over it. Well it was sure 'nough a bunch of dead people all standin' there not doin' nothin'. Usual I woulda been more muddled by seein' them dead people but instead I was kinda curious. I mean this was a lot more interestin' that what was goin' on around me in that Indian village.

Pretty soon some of them dead people started movin' around a little bit. First they'd move their arms and then their heads. One or two of 'em started walkin' a little ways but they walked in kinda circles and didn't go nowhere. Eventual all of them dead folks started walkin' around and lookin' at each other but no one said nothin'. They just walked and walked. Well this was gettin' to be no more interestin' than the little hut and the yard and them Indians chantin' and drummin'. I was about to try to think of somethin' else when of a sudden all them dead people turned at the same time and looked right at me. Then they all raised up their right arms and pointed at me. Well I like to have gotten the shakes from that! It was like they was blamin' me for somethin', and I never done anythin' to any of 'em. Then I think maybe they is thinkin' I should join up with them, but I wasn't anywhere near to do doin' that!

Just about the time I tried to figure out some way to see somethin' else in my muddled brain all those dead folk started to get smaller and smaller. Eventual they just kinda shrunk away to nothin' and my brain had a blank picture again.

That's when I decided I needed somethin' else to eat so's I fixed myself another one of them dinners of flat bread and beans. I had forgot to soak anymore strips of squash so I just put about four of them in mouth one at a time and let them soak up my spit and then I'd chew them. Trouble is that food made me sleepy again, and the drummin' and chantin' had not be goin' on for a while.

I figured I didn't have too much longer to last without sleep, so I started walkin' around in my little yard to stay awake and that worked out pretty good. Then another one of them muddled brain things happened. As I am walkin' I see another human bein' in my yard. This person was a man some bit taller than me who looked to be about two times my age. I walked over to him thinkin' that he wasn't real, but I was wrong. He was still there. I didn't try to touch him or anythin' like that 'cause at this time I was lookin' for some company and didn't want him to disappear.

Well damn, excuse me ma'm, if he didn't start talkin' to me. Here is what I remember him sayin': "Every sacred place must have guardians. If there are no guardians then anyone could enter even people who do not share the spirit of the place. Temples and cathedrals are guarded by gargoyles of all sorts. So you will know that you have entered a sacred place if you see guardians at the entrance."

*Editor's Note: Whoever recorded and transcribed this material apparently made an effort to have this figure not speak in O'Leary's manner and form. Presumably O'Leary did talk in his usual way while quoting what the figure had said.*

Well that sure was a peculiar thing to talk about to me standin' in my little yard which didn't seem like much of a sacred place and I sure didn't see any gargoyles anywhere. Of course, I weren't sure what gargoyle ought to look like neither!

Next thing I know this fella is gone. He was sure a kinda idea in my brain and not real, I figure. While he was there he seemed to be a right educated person like some important teacher. Since I never had no real education and never learneded to read or write, I wouldn't know about such things as educated people. Everythin' I have learneded I have learneded on my very own by bein' out in the world. I do admit to watchin' what other folks have done as in huntin' and fishin' and such. Most of my learnin' has been by makin' mistakes and then not makin' the same mistake again.

While I was thinkin' along those lines there was of a sudden another human bein' standin' in my yard but way on the other side of the yard. This was another fella. He seemed like he was real young, maybe half as old as me. No, I guess even younger than that. He was maybe just a striplin'. What they call green behind the ears. Now he come over to me, I didn't have to go to him. He looks me over real good, and the he says somethin' like this: "Mr. O'Leary, sir," he starts out, and I have never had anyone call me Mr. O'Leary sir in my whole life! "Mr. O'Leary, sir, you have traveled all over this Arizona territory as I have heard. I sure would be beholden to you if you would tell me the grandest thing or things you have seen in your travels. I would like to see those same things. However, sir, I do not have very long to live. I have the consumption as you may tell from how skinny I am. I believe I may have only a half year or year to live but would like to travel to see the most wonderful things there are in the Arizona Territory." Well now this muddled me old muddled mind even more! See I believed this was a real young boy standin' there, and I wanted to do right by him.

So I tell him first the about the canyons of the Colorado River, the big Colorado River but also the real narrow and deep canyon of the Little Colorado River right close to where it comes into the Big Colorado. Then I tell him also about the big mountain down south that stands near to the ponderosa forest. That mountain is so tall it mostly has snow on it in the winter time. It is some fifty miles or so south of the Colorado River canyons. Then I had to stop and think for a little bit 'cause those was the most wonderful things I had ever seen.

After a couple of minutes I remembered about the big cactus down in the desert, and I told him about them cactus and the fact that they had arms stickin' out of them and sometimes looked like old people standin' there. Except some of them had more arms than people do, by that I mean they had more than two arms. Well and the one other thing I could tell him about was that comin' up from the desert you climbs up what might seem like a mountain but it ain't. Instead it is a great long place that has risen up out of the ground higher than the desert and there's places on that thing that you can stand and you can see for what seems like a thousand miles. Well, you could only actual see for maybe a hundred miles on a good day. But it sure is a fair sight!

So those were the four things I told him to see: the canyons of the Colorado Rivers, the big mountain south of the canyons, them funny cactuses in the desert, and that great long high country from which you can see for many miles. He seemed real appreciative of my thoughts. And he thanked me real good for that. He also just got up and disappears.

What I come to think after he left me was that I had seen a lot of real wonderful things in my life but had never really noticed them. I had walked through them and seen them but never stopped to think on 'em. So that boy done me a great service, and I kinda swore to myself that I would go back and see all them things again. And maybe more. And in them next times I would take some time to actual notice what I was seein' instead of bein' ready to move on to somethin' else.

Now I could see some amount of light in the east so it musta meant it was close to mornin'. Which it turned out it was. I fixed me another one of them dinners which by now was gettin' to be pretty much of no great taste or interest to me. But I figured I needed to eat somethin'.

About middle of the mornin' on that second day the old man comes into my yard and looks at me. I am so muddled in my brain that at first I think he is my old Daddy from when I was a child. Then I see who it is. He makes a sign like I should go to sleep. Which I did right on the spot. Later that day I went into my little hut and slept some more. By late afternoon I had slept enough and come out of my hut. There was a party of them Indians sittin' in my yard, and they very kindly escorted me out of there into the village where some of them Indian ladies had fixed me a real meal with meat and everthin'. I ate most carefully not wantin' to upset any of them Indians, the ladies or the men. Once I was done eatin' I got real sleepy again, and they saw that. So they got me back to my little hut where I laid down and did not wake again until mornin'.

# How I Met the Changing Woman

**Now this is the only** way I can talk about the next thing that happened. They came and got me and walked me across that little village to a bigger house, I guess you could call it a house 'cause it was bigger than any of the huts, and they opened the door to it. They pushed me inside and closed the door. Now this house was real different from any Indian house I had ever seen. The walls was made of mud and timbers and went up I would guess twelve feet or more. They was way above my head!

Inside this part of the house there was another little house. But it was still bigger than the little hut I was in all the time. Somehow they got a lot of light into the big house. There was holes in the walls and holes in the roof. So it made it real light.

In all that light I could see six young Indian women, and they was all real beautiful! I mean they had that long black hair and dark eyes just like they all do. But they was real beautiful. I mean that in an Indian way. They wasn't beautiful in a White woman way. I been around Indians enough to know what is good looking in an Indian woman.

Them six young women come over to me and looked me over. It was what everbody in that whole tribe did to me! I begun to get a little upset over that. It was like I was some kind of odd little fella that they woulda had in a circus or carnival and someone would be hollerin' "Come look at the funny little man we found!" Well wasn't nothin' I could do about it. They had me, and right now there was no way I was goin' to get away from there.

Then one of them young women took my hand, and that was the first time that I could remember any of them touching me at all. She took my hand and straightaway led me over to a door in the smaller house. The one inside the bigger house. Then she kinda pushed me inside like I was a dog or steer or somethin'.

Inside that little there was a older woman. She real good lookin' too. Just older than the women on the outside of he little house. When I came in she was sittin' on the floor on some kind rug, and there was a rug in front of her. She pointed to the rug like I was supposed to sit there which I did. We was only about three feet apart, and I could see her real good because there was a lot of light in that little house. I couldn't figure out how it could be light 'cause there didn't seem to be any holes or windows or anything. And that door I had come through was shut tight.

It was like we was somewhere other than where we were. That don't sound right. But that's the way it felt. If there was a place that was the beginnin' of the world then that is how this place felt. It weren't in the Arizona Territory but somewhere else. It were somewhere that no one had ever been! That's how I honest felt when I was in that room with that woman.

I felt like I was somewhere real strange in front of some woman who was beautiful but kinda strange at the same time. I never felt like she was anyone I would want to be with, if you know what I mean, ma'm. She was more like a person who could be like a mother to me except she wasn't like my Mama. But she seemed like she could take care of you if you needed bein' taken care of. When I looked again at her still lookin' at me, I seen someone who coulda been my sister if I had had a sister, which I didn't. It was someone you wanted to know and maybe be a older brother too. You know someone you could kinda protect and take care of. But then my whole way of knowin' changed again so's she seemed like a person who could be your friend. Kinda like someone you could trust. I woulda been able to go out in the desert or mountains with her and feel real comfortable that she would be able to carry her part of the load. Like a partner. Except I never had no partner and never wanted or needed one. I like doin' things my own way without havin' to take into account what someone else would want or need. So I seen this woman as my mother and then my sister, which I never had, and then a partner. Come to think of it the last part she coulda been my brother which I did have but he didn't like me and I didn't like him 'cause he done some dirty deals to me when we was young men. But this woman woulda been a good brother.

Then of a sudden this woman stops looking at me and raises her head up and looks straight up at the roof of that little house. Now this is where it got very strange for me. This woman who was beautiful when I come in all of a sudden started changing her way of seemin'. I seen her eyes kinda sink back in her head, and her skin started to wrinkle up. I mean all over her face not just around her eyes or mouth. All that time her hair was also changin' so it become kinda wild, kinda as if she had been in a big wind. I once heard of old women in some play that a person told me were hags, and this is kinda how this woman was lookin' now. She was a hag. I mean she looked real mean, and I didn't want to be anywhere close to her even though I was sitting right there in front of her. I ain't been scared many times in my time but this time I was right scared. More than when I had faced a bear one time in them Rocky Mountains or when a big old rattlesnake was sittin' right next to my bedroll in the desert one day!

About as soon as I seen her change that way she started changin' again. That scared almost as much as her bein' a hag! This time her face and hair changed back to where they had been but somehow she appeared to me to be kinda slidin' away from me even though I believe there was the same distance as had been. Now she didn't look at me at all. It was like she was gone. I mean she was not there! I don't know how she did that, but she was just plain gone! This was the damndest thing, excuse my language, ma'm. I might as well have been in a empty room instead of in that room with that woman. Right then I wanted to reach over and maybe snap my fingers or even touch her to see if she would come back. But I couldn't do that, not in the situation in which I found myself. Who knows what woulda happened if I had done one of those things. So I just sat about as muddled as I had been the whole time while she started changin'.

So I was sittin' there with this woman who was there but wasn't there for a while and then she started changin' again. This one was even worser than anything had gone before. This woman started gettin' bigger and bigger. I do believe she was really gettin' bigger, and it wasn't just my imagination. Now this room we was in wasn't all that big, and this woman started fillin' up her side of the room, the back part away from the doorway. Well I figured if she kept gettin' bigger and bigger to the point where she filled up most of the room I would either die of lack of air or else I would have to scoot my way back to the door and out of there. Pretty soon she more or less filled up all the space my eyes could see. But she never got fatter or uglier. Just bigger and bigger. eventual she kinda loomed over me like a big cloud does in the sky.

I was ready to scramble out of that room no matter what it would mean, even if I had to die at the hands of them Indians, whatever kind they were. It was like I had smoked some of that peyote weed I had heard about or et some of them mushrooms the Indians in the south part of the Arizona Territory are supposed to eat. They get all kind of strange things they see that ain't real in the real world but are real to the people doin' the smokin' or eatin'.

Just as I was ready to skedaddle out of there, this woman starts shrinkin' to what should be her regular size, so I decide not to try to get away. I decide to wait and see what happens next. I mean I seen this woman be a regular kind of Indian woman when I come in even if she stared at me a lot but then she changes into a hag and then into a kind of ghost what ain't there and then into this huge being what growed to fill a whole half of the room. That would be enough to make any man go crazy or think he was crazy. That's what I thought at that time.

So we sit for a while, and I'm not sure how long. It was maybe part of a hour. I don't know. Then this woman stands up and uses her hands and arms to tell me to stand up. Which I do, of course, 'cause I don't want any trouble at this time since I was still alive and hadn't been eaten yet. She come over to me and she looked me right in the eyeballs the way that old man had done on top of the butte. But this was way different. I seen somethin' real strange in her eyes. They was like holes that you could see into. It scared me somethin' fierce 'cause I had never seen eyes like that before. It was true strange!

Then this woman she puts her hands on my shoulders, and I never felt like that since my dear old Mama used to come up to me when I was a real little child and do the same. Now I wasn't so scared even if she kept lookin' at me with those kinda empty eyes. There was some kinda good thing comin' outta her hands on my shoulders and it made me feel real good. Like I felt the whole damn world was good right then. Then I looked into her eyes again, and I swear I seen my old Mama or someone like her in them eyes. They looked just like my Mama's eyes when I was a young thing.

It was like my whole body was feelin' real good. I don't mean like bein' with a women or afterward but real relaxed and good feelin'. I could feel my whole body all at once, and I never felt that before. Everythin' felt good. It was like I had just been borned as a adult person. Felt like I just come to life right there.

That just kinda pleased and scared me at the same time, ma'm. It was good to feel that good, but it was bad to have never felt it before. So's I was in one of my mind muddles, but it didn't matter because of the feelin' so good.

Then somethin' happened that I never expected, and I don't ever want it to happen again. I started cryin' like a li'l child! I ain't cried in many a year. The last time was one of the whuppin's my Daddy gave me for doin' something bad. After that I never cried again no matter how much the whuppin' hurt. Soon after I left my home and my sweet Mama just to get away from them whuppins'. And I never had anything after that happen that would make me cry. So here I was where nothin' happened, and I was cryin'. Well I tell you I was embarrassed from my toes to the top of my head for bawlin' like a little newborn calf.

That woman she just held onto my shoulders. She didn't try to hug me or comfort me. She just held me there. I cried for what musta been some minutes before I could stop. And I tell you I did try to stop! When it was all over I felt somewhat better but still ashamed of myself for cryin' like that. Finally she just pats me on the head like I'm some little kid and walks away.

So I turn around and walk out of there. Strange thing is that there weren't no wet on my cheeks nor tears in my eyes in just a minute after that woman left. Still don't know what happened!

What I come to learn from that time with that woman was that there is a lot of different ways in which a woman can be a woman which I had never thought about afore. Mostly I had thought a woman was someone you was with, if you know what I mean, ma'm. 'Course I knowed about my old Mama, and that I wouldn't lay with her, no way. I come away from that time with the woman almost regrettin' that I had not spent more time with some women 'stead of wanderin' around the Arizona Territory.

# *How I Spent Three Days Alone on a Butte with No Food*

**After that meetin' with what** I called Changin' Woman, I was left pretty much to do as I pleased includin' walkin' around the village. Them Indian People was very nice to me even if we couldn't exactly talk to each one and another. The women would let me watch their work as they ground corn and soaked them dried squash slivers and all that. I seen them soaking the corn so's to help make the corn mush that they later used. At least I think that is what they did.

It was gettin' on into what we White folk call early October by this time, and the sun was right warm and friendly each day without gettin' too darn hot. From down there in the village you could see a whole mess of buttes around, but I couldn't see that big black rock no more. It was somewhere behind where we was and maybe behind one of them buttes.

I was also gettin' to know a few of the words in their language like I knew the words for corn, squash, and beans, but I can't remember 'em now. There was some other words I could learn by pointin' at stuff and havin' them say the word. They was always willin' to do that which made me feel more at home. About this time I started thinkin' about goin' on to the San Juan River like I had always planned but on the other side of that coin I wasn't too sure about leavin' or whether they would let me. I figured there was more villages between where I was and the San Juan River so's I would have to get past them villages and the folks in this village prob'ly had told some of the others about me. I didn't feel exactly trapped or like I was in a jail but then I didn't feel total free either. Which was kinda strange considerin' the kind of the life I had been livin' up to this time. I mean I was always free to go wherever I wanted and whenever I wanted which was the way I wanted.

One day while I was wanderin' around the village I seen this man walkin' towards me and some other Indians, and I had not seen him before. I kinda watched as he come to the village. That's when one of them Indian men folk tried to tell me somethin' about him. There was a lot of gesturin' goin' on. I tried to figure it out but couldn't at that time. Finally one of them Indian women she tried to show me more dramatic like. She pretended to feel a lot of pain with groanin' and pretend cryin'. Then she lays down on the ground and is like she is almost dead. That's when she point to this man who is still walkin' toward the village and points to her insides. All of a sudden she is feelin' better and able to sit up. From that I figure out this man must be their Medicine Man. The I figured out that he was the same man what come up to me back when we was around that Big Black Rock just afore they took me up there. So's then what he did kinda makes sense in its own way.

Now he was dressed somewhat different from the other folks and had on him some bracelets and other things and there was some things I didn't recognize hangin' from his shirt. Also he carried a little bag which prob'ly held his medicines that he used to cure folks.

What was strange then was that he come right up to me and like everybody else who had come up to me he looks me over real careful includin' lookin' right into my eyes. Well 'cause of that I could look right into his eyes but they was a total blank. They was dark and showed me nothin'. Then he starts sayin' some kinda prayer or chant over me which makes me feel real strange, and my poor old brain starts gettin' all muddled again. While I was able to walk around the village and just watch folks my brain was not at all muddled, but now it started up again.

Then that Medicine Man held a kind of meetin' with some of the other Indian men. There was a lot of slow talkin' and gesturin'. When they was done the Medicine Man comes over to me and tries to tell me somethin'. He sees it is not workin' so he stoops down and starts drawin' pictures in the dirt. I stooped down alongside him to see what he was drawin'. The first picture was of one of them buttes. Then he points to me and to the top of that butte. Well I figured he was tryin' to tell me something about when they brought me up that butte some time ago. But then he draws a picture of three big jars like they use for carryin' and storin' water and another picture of what looks like my bedroll! Next he does a interestin' thing in that he draws a picture of a man which I guessed was me and has that man walk up to the butte and then walk up the side of the butte to the top. Now I ain't ever walked up the side of anythin' so that didn't make sense to me. What he seemed to want me to know was that I was goin' to go to a butte somewheres. Final he does the same thing as that other fella some time before and draws three suns with a line in between each of 'em. So I understood that they wanted me to go to the top of one of them buttes for three days with three jars of water.

At this time I draw what I think are some pictures of food like corn and beans. The Medicine Man just scratches them out. I ain't gonna have no food for three days, I guess. That ends our little talk, if that could be called a talk.

The Medicine Man leads me back to my little hut and points to my bedroll which I make back into a bedroll 'cause it was all laid out to sleep on. When we come out of the little hut there is a regular posse standin' there with three of them Indian men carryin' the big jars of water which musta weighed quite some bit. So we start walkin' out of the village, and now I can see there is a butte not too far away but it don't seem to have no trail up it. In fact there don't seem to be no way to get up that thing! Turns out that was not the butte I was goin' to. There was another one futher off, and that is where we headed.

This one was somewhat bigger but not any taller. We kept on walkin' over to that bigger butte and sure 'nough there was trail right up the side of that thing although you wouldn't have knowed it from standin' anywhere around it. Only them what's been here for a while woulda knowed where it was. Now when I say it was a trail, I mean it was a skinny little old thing what wasn't much bigger than my two feet side alongside. Me, I just started up there and kept my eyes on that skinny old trail and didn't dare look down at all. I do not know how them Indian men carryin' them jugs of water ever got up there! I truly don't.

Once we got to the top they just kinda signed me that I was too stay up here for a while, and they put them three jugs of water down next to me. Then all of them walked on over to where the trail started down and before I knowed it they was gone.

After they left me up there I picked a place where I thought I might be able to sleep somewhat, and it was nowhere near the edge of that butte! I didn't want to be rolling over in the nighttime and fallin' down a couple hundred feet or more to the desert down there. There was a small hollow in the rock about in the center of that butte, and that's where I put my bedroll down. One thing I knowed from walkin' around a lot is that you can sleep better on rock or hard sand if there is a hollow so's you're head is a little higher than the rest of you. Sometimes, if the hollow is somewhat short, your feet also end up higher.

Then it come to me that maybe I could just get back down that trail in the mornin' and head for the San Juan River which is where I wanted to be. So I walked to the edge of that butte where the trail was, and I seen that they had left a young Indian man there so's I could not run away. Well that that all right. I could always get to the San Juan River, someday I guessed. Might as well sit back and see what happens on this butte.

Thing is, ma'm, I been journeyin' all alone most of my life so bein' on that butte alone didn't seem all that bad at first. And there has been times when I have been without food for a period, maybe a day or two. That's prob'ly which I'm so skinny. Anyway I sudden like realized that it was one thing to walk around the Arizona Territory all alone 'cause there was always things to see and do, and you had to figure out where to put your bedroll down so's you'd be comfortable and safe and so on. Well walkin' around the top of that butte was a whole different thing. After a couple hours I knowed every nook and cranny in the top of that butte. There wasn't anythin' new to find or see. Same as lookin' out from the butte. Pretty soon I had seen everythin' there was to see. So I was goin' to spend three days up there without a heck of a lot to keep me busy. Then I made up my brain to just settle in and rest up a great deal. Which I did. That first day went real slow and I final went to sleep right about the time the sun went away.

Now I don't regular dream when I is walkin' around the Arizona Territory. By the time I put my bedroll down and eat a bit and then lay down after walkin' I get to sleep real good and don't wake up until it gets light out. That's a bit before actual sunrise, ma'm, just to let you know. Of course sometimes I got to get up in the night for you know what, ma'm. but I won't talk about that.

That first night I lay me down when it gets pretty dark, there again being no moon and just them stars above. I ain't real tired but there's nothin' else to do so I lay down. I do fall asleep pretty fast, I believe, 'cause of course you can't remember when you falled asleep 'cause then you are asleep. At least that's what I have figured out.

Sometime durin' that night I did have me a dream that enough to scare a man to his own death! In this dream I am walkin' along in a arroyo like I did when I come up this way from the Little Colorado River. Now all arroyos wander back and forth. They is only occasional in a straight line. Fella once explained to me that when the water comes whippin' down the arroyo it hits one wall and bounces off that one and hits the one across from it. That water digs out the dirt on them walls as it bounces back and forth. And that how all them twists and turns happen.

So I'm walking down this arroyo which ain't too deep at first 'cause I can actual see over the edge of the thing as I am walkin'. But then the darn thing starts gettin' deeper. Not by much but a little at a time. Pretty soon I can't see over it anymore, but I keep on walkin'. Well it just keeps gettin' deeper and deeper and just keeps goin' on and on. Most arroyos, at least ones I had knowed, eventual end up spillin' out into a flat place or else they dump their water into a river. But this arroyo just keeps goin' on and on. Eventual it does become a canyon. But it is real narrow and the walls is made of dirt. Most canyons is cut through rocks, not dirt. Well I tell you my dream-brain started gettin' real muddled just like my real brain would if that arroyo was as I seen it in the dream. I did not like that arroyo which had no end and was gettin' deeper and deeper. Finally it got so deep that there was nothin' but a little bit of sky overhead and them enormous high dirt walls. That's when I woked up and found out that my real brain was as muddled as my dream-brain. All I knowed was I didn't ever want to get into a real arroyo like that!

When I woken up in the morning I reached over to where I usual kept my food right next to my bedroll but there weren't any food there. That's when I remembered that they had put me up on that butte without no food at all and in any way. I was a slight bit hungry so's I drank some water from one of them big jars and that settled my insides down a bit. I walked around the top of that butte about seventy hundred times it felt like but o' course I didn't get nowhere. All I could see was the same old buttes and desert that I had seen the day before and that I would see again and again as long as I was up on that butte.

Well there was so little to do I actual started to draw little pictures in the dirt on that butte just to pass the time. I kept thinkin' about when it would be time to eat again around noon and then had to remember myself that there weren't any food. At this time the sun was no longer real high in the sky 'cause it was approachin' late October as near as I could figure. As a matter of real fact it could pretty cold at night, but I was okay wrapped up in my bedroll. One of the things I had learneded while walkin' around the Arizona Territory and particular in the winter time was that you could keep yourself somewhat warmer if you wrapped somethin' around your head. Which I did. I once had a old knit cap that was real good for that, but it got lost or wore out somewhere along the way. So I started usin' a big old piece of flannel sheet that I had got from somewhere. I think maybe some kind woman in a town somewhere had give it to me. Anyways it worked real good when wrapped around my head. I even learneded how to wrap it kinda like them Arabs, at least like I seen them in pictures a few times 'cause I never seen a Arab up close anywhere in the Arizona Territory. They might have been some around, but I never seen them. Don't suspect there were any now that I think on it.

I put in a whole day of doin' nothin' which was about to get my brain real muddled again. As you may have found out, I don't like to have a muddled brain. But in this case I didn't have much choice. For a while I went over and sat on the edge of the butte with my legs hangin' over the edge which did make me feel a little funny in the guts. I never did like to be up high and look over the sides of a canyon or a mountain, particular when the sides was real steep. This time I done it 'cause I needed some kinda excitement.

By the time the sun went away I was actual pretty tired, but I don't know why. Compared to when I was walkin' around the Arizona Territory I had not done nothin' all day. Maybe that is what made me tired. So I laid down with that Arab thing wrapped around my head and looked up at them stars that night. Anyone ever been in the Arizona Territory or anywhere else out in the West knows that the stars shine real bright, and there is so many of 'em you can't even begin to count. I didn't try to count.

Someone once tried to teach me about the stars, and the ways in which they form pictures in the sky. Things like lions and bears and such. There is even supposed to be water carrier carryin' a big jug of water. Never could make any sense of all that. So now I just look up and let them stars shine on me without no thinkin'.

I did not sleep well that night, ma'm. It weren't the cold 'cause my Arab head wrappin' thing kept me nice and warm inside my bedroll. I guess it was just 'cause I had not done anythin' all day. I rolled to one side and then the other. I actual got up and walked around a bit which was no problem 'cause star light is enough to see by in the desert land like that.

Almost as good as one of them small moons, you know when it is just a part of the moon.

Final I did sleep and then started that dreamin' thing again. This time it was like a whole story that seemed to last for many hours. It was all about some kinda war that was bein' fought. Part o' the time I was in the middle of the fightin' though I didn't seem to have a rifle or nothin'. It was like I was just watchin' but from inside 'stead of outside.

That dream was real unsettlin' to me 'cause there were all kinds of men bein' killed and some o' them was bein' hurt but not dyin'. At least not dyin' real quick. They was layin' on the ground and moanin' and cryin'. Now I don't like it when growed men moan and cry. That is not real comfortin' to me. I would prefer that they would just die, but I guess that is a mean thing to say.

Well this battle goes on a long time with shootin' and hollerin'. Some of the men run at the other men while they was shootin'. Sometimes the men would lay down on the ground and shoot at the others who would also be layin' down. How they come to ever hit anybody I never did figure out. Maybe they didn't.

These men was dressed in different kinds of outfits. Some looked like they had just come out of the woods in deerskins. Others was dressed in fancy outfits that was red and blue and yellow. I mean some of the outfits was mostly red. Others was mostly blue. And some was mostly yellow. It was not like the War Between the States which I had seen pictures of where there was blue outfits and grey outfits. Nope in this war there was all kinds of outfits.

I seen the blue outfits shoot at the red ones, and then the yellow ones shoot at the red ones and blue ones. And the red ones seemed like they was shootin' at everybody maybe even some of the other red ones. The ones in deerskins spent most o' their time slippin' around and dodgin' bullets and didn't seem to shoot at anyone. It was a real muddled up war.

Then right at the end when it was hours after I started the dreamin' all of a sudden all the shootin' stopped. The men in all the different colors of outfits got up and damned if they didn't go up and shake hands with every one another. Blues shakin' hands with the reds, and the reds shakin' hands with the yellows. It was like they was sorry they had been shootin' at each other. Only trouble was there was all these bodies layin' around, mostly dead, but some certain number moanin' and groanin'. The folks in the fancy outfits paid no attention at all to the ones on the ground.

Well I ended up feelin' real bad about the whole thing like it was real. When I woken up from this dream, I felt like I didn't want to do nothin'. It was like there was a big heavy old piece of lead on my shoulders, and my brain would not work right no how.

I was complete woken up and sittin' there 'fore the sun come up. That day went real slow. There was nothin' to do, and I was gettin' to feel kinda weak in the body and the brain. It was like one of the times when I had some kinda disease when I was younger. I don't get much disease anymore now that I am older and don't know why. All I wanted to do that day was nothin' which seemed kinda sad but heck there weren't anythin' to do! I mean had walked that butte top what seemed like a many hundred times and knew just about every little old rock and stick and bush that was on it. Final I watched the ravens flyin' around over the butte and out beyond it. I just kept watchin' them ravens floatin' and then flappin' their wings. Sometimes they didn't do no flappin' and still got theirselves higher in the sky. Don't quite know how they did that. Ever once in a while one of 'em would swoop down on somethin' on the ground. Ravens usual do eat meat so they was lookin' for some kinda dead animal or bird on the ground.

That's when I come up with this idea that I would lay on the butte like some kinda dead human bein' to see if the ravens would come over to me. It was nice and warm and cool at the same time durin' that time of year on the butte so I could lay down just about any old where. Which I did. I laid me down on my back so's I could watch the ravens to see if any one of 'em would come over to me. Turned out to be somewhat fine to be layin' down like that with nothin' to worry about except for the fact that I truly wanted some food. However, I knowed there weren't goin' to be any food for another half day and then night.

Nothin' happened for what seemed like some long time, but then it was hard to tell how long I was layin' there 'cause I was always more likely to be movin' and I could tell time better when I was walkin'. Then sure 'nuf I seen a raven floatin' on over to the butte where I was layin', and that big old bird circled around over me and was lookin' me over. Final he put hisself right down about six feet from me and looked me over real good. He hopped in that funny way that ravens will hop when they is on the ground over closer to me. I am callin' this bird a 'he' 'cause I had no way of knowin' whether it was a boy or girl raven. Inside my brain I am sayin' "come on over here, Mr. Raven." 'cause I thought it would be real funny to have raven start peckin' on me. 'Course I wasn't quite dead yet so no raven would actual do that.

That raven stood absolute still and kept lookin' at me. The he cocks his head to one side like he is askin' me if I am alive or dead. Well I turn my head over to the side where he is and say "I ain't dead yet." Swear to God that old raven nodded to me. He squawked real loud almost right in my ear kinda like he was sayin' "You fooled me to come here when you weren't dead." Then he took off with that real noisy wing flappin' they do, and you can hear it loud if they is close enough.

So they weren't much else to do on that butte. I started wonderin' if maybe I could chew on my old leather belt to make me less hungry but final decided to get me another drink of water from one of them big jars. I did that and didn't feel hungry no more. I did not do much of anythin' the rest of that day but loll around and do nothin'. My brain was somewhat muddled again 'cause I thought I ought to be doin' somethin' but the didn't have no desire to do anythin'.

Final night came along after the sun went down which seemed to happen real fast that night. There was some clouds in the sky which I forgot to say early in my tellin' about this day. Them clouds kinda made it darker since it was hard to see the stars. I wrapped my head in that Arab thing and got into my bedroll.

Again I did not sleep well, and damned if that dreamin' didn't start up again. This time it was real clear like it was absolute real and not a dream at all. What I seen in that dream at first was the top of a butte somewhat like the one I was on. I was standin' in the middle of the top of that butte and buck naked! Sorry if that makes you feel muddled ma'm but that is the honest to God truth. Buck naked on a butte top with the sun shinin' and everythin'. But there was no people there to see me. I looked around me and couldn't see any clothes anywhere. It was like I had been put up there with no clothes 'cause if I had walked up with clothes they shoulda been around somewhere. One of the muddlin' things about these dreams is that I am thinkin' real clear about what is goin' on even when what is goin' on is real strange.

Next thing I know there is some people on that butte comin' to me but somehow I weren't too muddled about my havin' no clothes on. It seemed real natural which I guess it ought to be 'cause we was born with no clothes. Well these people come closer, and they is all smilin' and lookin' happy and come right up to me. They kinda looked me over which I didn't much appreciate 'cause I am kinda skinny and somewhat wrinkled from my age and bein' outdoors so much. They didn't seem to mind my bein' skinny and wrinkled. Then somehow they come up with some clothes for me which I don't know how they did 'cause they had not walked up with any clothes for me or anythin' that coulda held such clothes. Next thing I know I am standin' there in these real nice clothes which was like my regular walkin' clothes except much nicer. I mean they was real clean and pressed and not wrinkled either.

Seemed as how these folks wanted to help. I tried lookin' at them in this dream, and they didn't look like White Folks or Indian folks or Chinee folks or Negro folks or anything I had ever seen. They was just people which seemed kinda strange to me 'cause people ought to be of one sort or another. When I kept lookin' I knowed somethin' else which is that they was neither men nor women! They was all dressed the same and had the same kinda hair and all.

Next thing I know these folks which ain't any particular kind of folks and ain't men or women are helpin' me to get off the butte top. How we got off I do not know 'cause next thing I know we is down on some ground, and there is even some green grass and nice trees all around. Also there is a big table filled up with all kinds of food most of which I had never seen before. So we sit down and have ourselves a right wonderful meal all of which tastes real good to me even if I had never seen it or eaten it before. Ever one is bein' happy and smilin', but they is not talkin'.

After we is done eatin' some of these folks come over to me where I am sittin' at the table and they kinda move me over to another place but how they move me in that dream I did not know. I was just in another place. That is where some of them started rubbin' my shoulders and neck and makin' me feel real nice. All the while they is smilin' at each other and at me. I am thinkin' I ought to say somethin' to them, but they is still not talkin' so I figure I better do the same. Eventual they touch and rub me all over my body and that made me feel real good

The last part of that dream was real strange 'cause these folk got me to flyin' over the grass and trees and floatin' in the air like I was a raven or one of them big old buzzards. I could float along and then kinda lean to one side and turn real easy. This was real fun while it lasted. We didn't fly too long before I woke up from that dream, and the sun was rising up out of the east.

This was the third day I was up on that butte, and I figured I could come down off of it. Which I started to do and then seen that that Medicine Man was comin' to get me. Sudden like I was feelin' real hungry.

Well I tell you, ma'm, at the time I come off of that butte I didn't ever want to do any dreamin' again! I told my ownself that if that ever started happenin' again I would take me a big stick and whack my ownself alongside the head until it stopped. I never did dream no more while I was with them Indian folks and hope to never do it again.

# The Young Woman
# Who Come to Me

**After I come down off** that butte and at ate some of that Indian food which was not as good as the food I had dreamed of I was taken back to my little hut. I lived in that little hut for another some days, I don't remember the exact number because of the way my brain was all bunched up and wrong way around from the time with that woman in the big house and then on that butte. I lived in that little hut that was there and nothin' happened.

Then one evenin' just about sundown, I seen this young woman come through that gate into my place. She was real good lookin' but not one of the ones I had seen before. This was a different woman. Like all the others she had that long black hair and them dark eyes. But her skin was right smooth and almost shiny. I don't know how she got her skin to look like that.

What most got to me was she was dressed way different from all the other women. They all wore them long dresses, them deerskin dresses, that covered them from their shoulders all the way to below their knees. This woman was dressed a whole different way. Her dress kinda drooped in front and it was way short of the usual kind of dress I had seen. I could see her knees and even more.

Now excuse me here, ma'm, because I been with a few women in my life, if you take my meanin'. But I was never a man to go chasin' after women. The few times I was with a woman it seemed real nice. And it felt real good. But y' know it never lasted too long. It was like real short and then everything was just like it was before. I'm havin' trouble talkin' to you about this ma'm 'cause I ain't never spoke about it before to anyone not even another man. Anyways I spent most of my days out in the desert or the mountains and didn't need no contact with a woman. I was just as happy to be out walkin' and lookin' around and just tryin' to survive in this world.

So when this woman come into my place there in the desert in the Arizona Territories, I wasn't to sure about anything. I sure never asked for anyone like this to come to me. And I wasn't sure I wanted this woman to be there. She takes me by the hand and leads me into that little hut and shuts the door behind but leaves it just a crack open so's there'd be some light. Then she walks on over to my bedroll and sits down right on it and kinda gestures me to sit down there with her. Well I wasn't goin' to do that! No ma'm! So she gets right up again and pulls me down right next to her. Then she lays down there on my bedroll and pulls me down again so's we're layin' right next to each other.

This woman had no morals or somethin' 'cause she starts runnin' her fingers on my chest. I tried to get her to stop it but she wouldn't. Now I was getting real upset, and my brain was getting' all muddled up again. I guess it was that way for much of the time I spent with them Indians.

Next thing I know she is rubbin' my chest and looks right at me and smiles real big and pretty with shiny white teeth. You don't see too many of those Indians with shiny white teeth because of what they eat. I guess the young ones prob'ly have pretty white teeth 'cause they haven't ruint 'em yet. Anyway she smiles at me, and I know what is goin' on here, and I don't like it 'cause this young woman is someone's lover or some family's daughter and if they find out what she's doin' and tryin' to get me to do I coulda got in a peck of trouble! But she would not stop!!!

'O course I am a man, and all this is havin' the effect she wants on me. I mean my brain was muddled and now my old body was getting' muddled too, if you know what I mean, ma'm. I couldn't think straight the way a man gets in that kind of way when there is really only one thing you is thinkin' about.

Well then she stops all of a sudden and looks at me again with a smile. Now she gets up and pulls me up too so we're standing there. That's when she went back to the door and looked out. She must seen somethin' or nothin' because she comes back to me and kinda drags me to the door.

Sure 'nough there is no one around my place. I mean there was absolute no one! That's when she takes me by the hand again and walks me out of my little yard in front of the hut and out into the open. There is still no one could be seen anywhere around there.

Where in the heck she thought we was gonna go I do not know. But I guess she did. So still holdin' my hand, and it was like bein' held real gentle but certain, she leads me away from my little hut and away from where all the Indians was livin' in their huts. It is still light out, and we could see right easy where we were goin' and step over little rocks or around big ones and be careful when we come to little gullies where the water had run through. She kept walkin' until we was way out from the Indian village, and then she stops.

I knowed what was comin' next 'cause she stopped right next to a place where someone had made a bed of grasses and made it look real comfortin' like so's anyone with any tiredness would want to lay down there. And anyone with a muddled brain and muddled body like mine would want to lay down there with that young woman. Then she did what I thought she might and that is she started doin' a dance. She twirled around so's her dress kinda lifted up and showed more of her legs. She wiggled and waggled and danced, and it got me pretty much muddled up. I guess I could say I was getting' kinda excited and felt like I could maybe do that kind of dance too but I knew where that was goin' to lead.

So ma'm, I bolted just like a horse that's seen a rattlesnake. I turned myself about and headed back for where I thought that Indian village was and left that young woman back there. She come runnin' after me a little ways but I was runnin' from bein' afraid and she was runnin' for some other reason. It's real easy to run real fast when you is scared.

I did fall down one time from not watchin' where I was goin' but by that time she was nowhere to be seen. I made it back to my little hut and got inside there and waited. But she never showed up again. I know what is right and wrong, and I knowed that what that young woman wanted to do with me was wrong 'cause there weren't no love or any kind of understandin' atween us. Not to say I didn't want to be with her, but it was straight out and absolute wrong.

Strange thing is that I never seen her again the whole time I was with them Indian folks. It's like she almost weren't real. But then most of what I seen and heard and otherwise experienced didn't seem real either.

# *How the Medicine Man Showed Me About the World*

**After that young woman come** got me and took me out to that grass bed place, I was more or less left alone for a while which I did not mind. I have always walked alone in the Arizona Territory, so bein' alone is not strange at all to me. My brain is less muddled when I is alone than when there are other folks around with all their talkin' and tryin' to get you to do things.

Then about two-three days after the young woman come and my brain is less muddled and my old body is much less muddled. I was sittin' with my back against the outside wall of my little hut that day, and I was in the sun 'cause the night before had become somewhat colder. Cold enough that I wanted to be warm that day. Then I seen that Medicine Man fella walkin' into my little yard. He sits down right next to me.

As I had said before this Indian fella was dressed different from the others what with things hangin' off of him and all. Strange but this time he didn't seem to want to talk to me which I couldn't understand anyway, and he didn't try to draw any little pictures on the ground. He just sat next to me soakin' up that good mornin' sun. We both set there and just kinda enjoyin' the sun.

After a while this Medicine Man turns to me and say somethin' which again I don't understand. Anyway he keeps talkin' even though I don't understand. Eventual he gets up and signs to me to get up. Then he goes into my little hut, which I kinda didn't like 'cause by now it was my little hut and I didn't fancy anyone else goin' in there. Next thing I know he's got my bedroll in his arms, and it is all rolled up liked it should ought to be. With that he signs me to follow him which I had no choice but to do.

I was thinkin' that this was going to be another one of them things where I don't get to sleep or have to sit on a butte for three days, but I was wrong. This Medicine Man starts walkin' out of the village, and then I seen a adobe house, kinda made out of some rocks and mud but there was also sticks in the walls and it had a roof made of some wood beams covered over with brush and mud. And that's where we were goin'. So he's takin' me to his house which is kinda strange to my way of thinkin'.

When we get to this Medicine Man's house he shows me inside, and there is three-four rooms in there. It was a lot bigger inside than I had thought. Those rooms were separated out with wood stick walls which was not too thick but did serve to kinda screen off a person in one room from another. I would not call it great privacy though.

That Medicine Man goes into one of the rooms and puts my bedroll in there and then signs to me that it was my room which I kinda figured out anyway. He don't want me to go in there yet, I find out, 'cause he signs to me to come back outside.

Then we start walkin' around this house of his until he sees a big black beetle crawlin' along the ground. He points to it and the makes a couple more signs which I still don't understand. Final he points to the beetle and then to the sky where there is a few of them real skinny clouds. He points to the beetle again and then to the clouds and then he pretends like it is rainin' using his hands to show me rain. So I guess there is some hookup between the beetle and rain. I do the same what he did. I point to the beetle, point to the sky, and then make rainin' signs. He nods.

That was just the start of what I final figured out was a way to learn me some things that I had never knowed before. It was all about the dirt and beetles and other bugs and snakes and lizards and the sky and clouds and from which way the wind would blow. I had been outdoors a great deal in my walkin' through the Arizona Territory but I never paid much mind to them kinds of things. If it rained I found me a place to get away from it. If it were too hot, I would find some shade. If the wind blowed from the west or the east, I didn't much care so long as it didn't kick up too much dust.

One thing he showed me a couple of times was that you could kinda tell which way the wind was goin' to blow in the next hour or so or even the next day by lookin' at the kinds o' clouds there was in the sky. Them skinny clouds usual meant a wind from the west, maybe northwest or southwest. And there was goin' to be some kinda change in the wind and maybe even the weather. Big built up clouds that was dark underneath meant the wind would come from the north, at least in the winter.

Now I spent the better part of November with this Medicine Man and found out all about the ways in which beetles and spiders and such will tell you what time of year it is. O' course you can also tell that from where the sun comes up and sets down. But the beetles and spiders and such will tell you in some way when it is likely to turn a whole lot colder or warmer.

Then come December when the sun was real low toward the ground almost all day, this Medicine Man walks around and shows me some of the kinds of plants and grasses that was growing there in that desert. Now you may think, ma'm, that there's not much growin' in the desert but if you look close you can see a lot more than you would've thought. We picked some of the dry leaves of some plants and the seeds of others and took 'em back to the Medicine Man's house. Turns out they all have some use for the Medicine Man in makin' people feel better.

One thing he did that was real interestin' was that he would pick a bunch of sagebrush and take it back to the house. When we was there for a while he would take that sagebrush and tied it up tight with some grass that he had also brought back. Then he would hold that sagebrush over the fire in his house until it started to burn but then he would blow out the fire so the sagebrush was just a smolderin'. That Medicine Man would wave that around hisself and then around me and it smelled real good. He tried to tell me somethin' about that like it was some kind of Indian ceremony, but I didn't rightly understand what he was sayin'. I think it had somethin' to do with feelin' good and maybe keepin' bad things away. Anyways that's what I got from his signing.

Ever once in a while this Medicine Man would go from his house to the village, and I would follow him along to see what he would do. When he got to the village some of them Indian folks would gather up around him, and he would talk to them. They would all nod. I think he was tellin' them that he had found out somethin' about the days and nights or the winds or whatever.

It was real interestin' to watch this Medicine Man and all that he did most of which I still did not understand. But I decided to live with him some more even when the winds got real cold, and that old sun just barely warmed us up and that was only when it was around the middle of the day. Some days there was snow blowin' across the desert, and I tell you them buttes looked real pretty with snow on top of them and even layin' in the cracks down the sides. They looked somewhat like fancy cakes I had seen once in a town down south in the Arizona Territory. Most of the time the snow just blowed right across the desert and off to I don't know where and if it did stick to the ground it was usual melted off by the middle of the day or maybe the day after.

Sometime after what I figure was December or maybe early January that Medicine Man starts goin' outside early in the mornin' every day, and he sits there lookin' to the east. It was like he was waitin' for the sun to rise up. And that is exact what he was doin'. He showed me one mornin' just as that sun come up where it came right over a butte some miles away. In fact, it come up right alongside that butte. Then he did somethin' strange which was strange to me but eventual worked out real interestin'. He took himself a pretty straight stick and stuck it right straight up in the dirt. That stick is makin' a shadow which that Medicine Man then draws in the dirt with another stick so's when the sun moves there' still be a line there. Then that Medicine Man and me we go back to his little house away from the Indian village and do some chores and we even took a short sleep 'cause it was winter and somewhat cold outside. It felt real nice to roll up in my bedroll in the middle o' the day and just lay there and maybe just fall just a slight amount asleep.

That afternoon as the sun was settin' that Medicine Man points to me and then outdoors, and we go back to that stick in the ground. 'Course now the sun is way over in the west and castin' another shadow with that stick. That Medicine Man then draws a line in the first just like he did in the mornin', and damned if the two lines don't match up exact they was both bent the same amount and in the same way. So's they kind made a teepee lookin' thing though these people did not make teepees which was only made up north by some other Indians. Them two lines also looked like one of them pyramid things they got in Egyptian land. That Medicine Man then sat down there wrapped up in his blanket somethin' which I had not brought along so I went back to the house and got one o' my blankets and come back figurin' that Medicine Man had something to learn me. Indeed he did, ma'm. While I had been goin' to get my blanket that Medicine Man had drawed an entire second line straight up and down from them other lines t so it pointed mostly north and south did that second line which I thought was real interestin'. I did not know why we was still sittin' there. Soon as it got kinda dark, and that Medicine Man he gets up and goes over to the lines in the dirt and points to me to come over which I do. Then he points to the second line, the one that was a north-south line, and then he points up in the sky and there was that North Star that most of us who lived outdoors a lot have come recognize real easy. That Medicine Man then made some sounds that was the name of the North Star which I do not remember any more.

Well that Medicine Man got up ever' mornin' and sat there and watched the sun come up so I got to where I would get up with him and also watch. The sun come up at a little different place ever' mornin' which I kinda knowed but had never watched real close before. Ever' mornin' he got up and looked real close where the sun come up against a butte or some big rock or some other thing he could see. The one mornin' he got up and looked and he nodded his head and then he showed to me where the sun was risin' right over some notch in a small butte. That day later he went down to the Indian village and was tellin' them somethin' which turned out to be that they should start diggin' up the dirt nearby the buttes 'cause it was gettin' close to plantin' time. And that is how he figured out when to dig up the fields and later when to plant the beans and then the corn and final the squash. Since bein' with that Medicine Man I have never been any one place long enough to figure out how to look for the sun risin' in particular places so I could not put that teachin' to any great use. But it was real interestin'.

The thing I did final figure out was that when that Medicine Man went in to the Indian village it was always to tell them Indian folks somethin' about what was happenin' like with the weather or the sun risin' in the right place or maybe with the ground. In the spring time I did see the Medicine Man keep lookin' at the ground all the time, and I couldn't figure out what he was doin'. He would look down and even get down on his knees so's he could more clearer whatever it was he was lookin' for. That went for a several weeks after he told them Indian folks to start diggin' up their fields. Now I went with him most mornins' 'cause I was real interested in what he was lookin' for. Then one day he leaned down real close to the dirt and kinda scraped at it with his one finger. I went down there right next to him, and what I seen was some little of them ant insects startin' to move around. I figured out eventual that them ant insects would start crawlin' around when the dirt got warm enough and that was what that Medicine Man was waitin' for. That day he went on into the Indian village and told them Indian folks to start plantin' for sure. So the way he worked all that out was between the way the sun come up and how the ground was warmin' up.

One thing that happened was that I learneded some words in the language of these Indian folks. They was mostly the names of things like beetles and other bugs. I learneded the names of the winds 'cause they had a different word for each kind of wind. I think that was 'cause they didn't have the notion of north, east, south, and west as the White folk do. They knew where the sun come up and set down at times of the year. And they could point to what we call the North Star. But when it come to tellin' about the wind, they had a different name for each one. Same for clouds, but I don't know that us White folk have any names for clouds or if we do I sure have never heard them spoke. There was names for the buttes and the arroyos and other kinds of places in their land. I do believe they even had names for partic'lar buttes where they lived.

So I could get up in the mornin' and point to a cloud and give it the right Indian name which made that Medicine Man seem somewhat happy. Although I never seen him actual smile.

One day I tried to ask that Medicine Man a question 'cause I had noticed that he did not live in the Indian village with the Indian folks. That seemed real strange to me since what he did was real important to them Indian folks. Well I gestured and signed away and drawed a map showin' his house and the village and then I shrugged my shoulders at him which seemed to be a way to show I was wonderin' about somethin'. This went on for most of half a hour or so until I think he got the drift of what I was askin'. Then he started up gesturin' and drawin' things in the dirt that did not make a lot of sense to me so we went at it again for most of half a hour. I finally figured out that he lived away from the Indian village and the Indian folks 'cause it was easier for him to watch the sun and look at the ground and all them things he done without bein' bothered by a lot of folks around him. That made good sense to me 'cause I'd just as soon be off somewheres and not be too bothered by folks. I mean of course White Folks.

I coulda learneded a lot more from this Medicine Man if I had knowed more of his language, but still I learneded a lot I do believe. One thing I do remember real well is that my brain was not much muddled after spending those months with that Medicine Man.

# How I Met the Chief of the Tribe and What He Done to Me

**This part I had forgot** to tell you before, ma'm, and it shoulda been before 'cause all this about the Chief Man did happened before I went to live with that Medicine Man. Them Indian folks left me to do what I wanted pretty much for a while. I sometime thought about gettin' out o' that village and away from them Indian folks but it weren't a bad life around there. I mean they gave me enough food to live on real comfortable 'though I was kinda tired of corn mush, beans, and squash with sometime just a little bit of rabbit or some other meat which I did not recognize and did not want to know about. I even begun to think that maybe this would not be a bad place to live what with no work to do and all. However, it was way different from my usual way of livin' which was walkin' around the Arizona Territory to see things and occasional talk to some White folk in some town or settlement. I never had to make money no matter what 'cause there was always some food around that I could gather up or else some animal that I could hunt and butcher and then eat. So sometime I also thought about gettin' away from that village. Main problem with livin' there was that I had not learneded much of their language and sooner or later a human bein' needs to have some talk with another human bein' even if it real simple talk with not a lot of meanin'.

Then one day three-four of the men come to me and kinda showed me that I was s'posed to go with them which I did. This time we went to a hut near the middle of the village where I had never been too much. This hut was somewhat bigger than the rest of them but also made out of sticks with mud and a roof of wood beams, sticks, tree leaves, and then mud. Them men pointed to the door which was a good size like I was to go inside. Which I did. They followed me in.

Inside there was not much 'cept some men sittin' around, about ten or so of them, in a kinda half circle, and in the middle of them men was a man who was dressed different from the others. He had a lot fancier clothes and had all kinds of stuff hangin' off of them clothes which I checked real quick to see if there was any scalps but I did not see any. He pointed to the ground right in front of him where I was supposed to sit.

So I sat down there cross-legged like they was all sittin'. This man in the middle I figured was a chief or some such because of where he sat and the kind of clothes he had on and all that other stuff. Once I had sat down I was able to look more closely at him, and I sure have to say that he was ugly! There was not one good thing about his face that I could see, and I have seen some real ugly White men before. What was even worse he pulled back his lips like he was goin' to grin but he didn't grin and all I could see was his teeth which as all pointed like that of a wolf.

Now I don't scare real easy, but this man again made my brain muddled with some amount of fear. I would just as soon have gone out of there and back to my little hut but that didn't seem likely. Next thing I know this man, who is prob'ly somethin' like sixty or seventy years old from what I can see starts hollerin' and screamin' at me like I done somethin' wrong. Which I didn't think I had done at all. All them other Indian men are lookin' at me real stern somewhat like I had seen a couple of times when someone had got me to go to a church where the preacher was shoutin' things and there was men who looked just like these men except they was White. That's why I didn't go to too many churches of which there wasn't too many in the Arizona Territory anyway and particular in the places where I went.

Well this Chief man keeps on with his hollerin' and screamin' at me, and it don't mean nothin' to me since I don't understand what he is sayin'. I do know he was real mad at me for some reason, but as I said before I had not done nothin' wrong to my mind. after a while he stops and then just looks at me. That's when he stands up, and I see that he is maybe no more than five feet three tall and real skinny, at least he looks skinny inside those clothes.

Ever body gets up and I do the same and then we all walk outside the house. All them men are kinda in a circle around me as if I might try to run away. The Chief man keeps on walkin' until we is out of the village entire and in some open ground. He looks up at the sky where there is a few of them little white clouds that come up in the late summer and early fall. Pretty soon he is hollerin' and screamin' at the sky which seems funny to me except that the next thing I know some of them clouds are sorta gatherin' up together and become a bigger cloud that gets taller and also darker on the underneath side. Seems like it has become a storm cloud only from that Chief Man hollerin' at the sky which is somethin' I had never seen before. Not sure any White man coulda done the same.

Then them bigger clouds started showin' lightnin' and thunderin' like mad. One of the things that I have always knowed was that lightnin' was extreme dangerous. Once I seen the carcass of a steer that had been hit by lightnin', and it was just about total roasted from that lightnin' which must be extreme powerful. Also I have had other fellas tell me about persons who have been struck by lightnin' includin' one fella what was standin' next to a tree that was hit and that fella was struck dumb and never did talk again. He just kinda shook all over after that like it had muddled his brain total.

So that's why I was real concerned when that Chief Man takes me by the arm and kinda drags me towards where them clouds was and the lightnin' was hittin'. But he weren't goin' to take "no" for a answer and just kept pushin' and draggin' me over that way which was maybe a quarter mile. When we got closer there was even more lightnin' and that thunder was so loud it about broke my ears open! Pretty soon we was right in the middle of all that, and I figured we was goin' to die. Well we didn't. We just stood there in the middle of all that until that cloud moved away and then it fell apart and there was no storm anymore.

I had a real hard time figurin' out why that Chief Man wanted to take me out there where it was so dangerous and dangerous for him as much as me. About then is when I kinda regretted not havin' walked away from that village some time ago when maybe I had a chance.

The Chief Man he just looks at me and pulls back his lips and shows me them pointy teeth which don't do me no good at all. That man could not smile if God hisself came down and told him to!

Then we walked back to the village where I went back to my little hut but this time I did notice that they had put some of them Indian men around my place so's I wouldn't run away. I sure wanted to!

So I go into my little hut and try to figure out what in the heck that Chief Man was tryin' to do to me but my brain was so muddled I couldn't think of nothin'. So I laid me down and took at little sleep that afternoon which lasted until almost sunset. By this time a big old moon had come up and was shinin' bright and silvery like the moon will do.

Then there was a coupla days where no one did nothin' with me or to me for which I was real thankful. That only lasted a coupla days. Some of them Indian men come to me after my noon meal which again was mostly corn mush, beans, and some squash with a little bit of rabbit meat. So they motion me to come with them which I do, and we go back to the Chief Man's house. He is standin' there and walks out, and we head back up to that butte what's got the trail up it with maybe ten-twelve Indian men walkin' along with us.

When we get to the top o' that butte the Chief Man he goes over to the edge of that butte right on top where is there is a drop of prob'ly at least two hundred feet and lays himself down with his head towards the edge and his feet pointin' in towards the middle of that butte top. The rest of us is just watchin' when two of them Indian men they go up to the Chief Man layin' on the ground there and grab him by the ankles, and they hoist him as easy as can be. I figure he couldn'ta weighed more'n a hundred and maybe ten pounds. So they picks him up by the ankles. Next thing I know they is walkin' a coupla steps over to the edge of the butte with the Chief Man kinda between them upside down. Now this is one of the oddest things I ever seen. Then without thinkin' or stopping; or anythin' they walk right up to the edge of the butte top and dangle that Chief Man out there in the clear air over the edge a coupla hundred feet over the ground below. Well my whole insides start aquiverin' like they never had before as I didn't know if they was goin' to drop him or what but of course they wouldn'ta dropped their own Chief Man. He is danglin' between them just as peaceful as can be with his head pointed right straight down, and he's holdin' his arms right beside his body. Then them Indian men holdin' the Chief Man start kneelin' down so's to lower the Chief Man over the edge where there ain't nothin' but clear air down to the bottom. All them other Indian men are just lookin' without the least concern. After just a little while but what seemed a long while they hauled the Chief Man back up and set him down real gentle on the butte top which is when he got up and looked right at me.

That did not make me feel too good 'cause I had a feelin' about what was comin' next and sure enough two more o' them Indian men come over to me and walk me to the edge where I can see right straight down. The push me down on to the butte top dirt and grab my ankles at which time I figure they is either goin' to hoist me up and drop me over the edge or what else I don't know. Well they did hoist me up and dangled me over the edge of the butte top to where I was lookin' out beyond the butte and not towards it. Other words I could see a ways out there and a ways down neither of which made me feel good. Then they done to me what they done to the Chief Man which is the lowered me so's I was down below the top of that butte, at least most of me was. My insides was shakin' real good but I did not want them to know that so I tried to stay as still as possible and I held my arms right up against myself just like the Chief Man had done.

It seemed like a good long time before they hauled me back up which is what they did eventual. My brain was muddled and my body was as muddled as my brain but I did not let them know that! I was able to stand up almost by myself without the help of any of them Indian men although for a minute I was not able to walk at all.

After all that the Chief Man he just nods at me, and we walk back off that butte down the trail and back to the village. Them Indian men leave me by my little hut and walk away without nothin' else happenin'. This is when I felt a powerful need to get away from those Indian folks, but I was not able to 'cause of the guards they had posted near to my little hut.

After all them things the Chief Man made me do it come to me that he was kinda testin' me to see what I was made of. I guess I passed all them kind of tests which I could never have done with them school tests they give to the young folks. Particular since I cannot read nor write which makes it hard to pass them school tests. What happen to me, I believe, is that I come to kinda understand that sometimes it is all right to go ahead and let some other person like the Chief Man take over your life for a while so's you can come to be a better human bein'. Maybe even it is a good thing to understand that you can't, as a one person bein', have total rule even over your ownself's life.

I got up a lot of respect for that old man, the Chief Man, for what he made me do which he also did to his ownself. He was no spring chicken and prob'ly two times as old as me, and he still could do all that. Other thing I noticed after all that was that the Chief Man was not as ugly as I have original thought. He still had them pointy teeth which now didn't scare me at all. What I seen now was that what I thought original was ugly was only 'cause of all the things he had done and come through and been tested by.

When we was all done, at least I though we was all done, I wanted in some way to show my respect for the Chief Man which was hard 'cause I didn't know how they did that among them Indian folks. If he had been a White man I woulda shook his hand and maybe slapped him on the shoulder at the same time. But if I did that to the Chief Man it prob'ly wouldn't be good. I also seen the Chinee put their hands together and bow in front of their older men in a sign of respect, but this was no Chinee old man here. And if he was one of them military officers I woulda saluted him like they do. If he was one of them religious people I coulda kneeled down in front of him and pretended to be prayin' or some such. But he weren't no military officer or religious priest or Chinee old man and for sure no White man.

What I did final was just to kinda nod to him the way I seen some of their men do, and then I did somethin' real odd for me. I put my hand on my chest right over my heart which seemed kinda girlish. But the Chief Man did the same, so I figured that was all right.

And that was the way we left it.

# *What I Come to Realize*

**I spent considerable time in** that village after all that stuff with the Chief Man and ever once in a while I seen him. He always nodded to me and I did the same back to him. It was like he knowed somethin' about me which maybe I didn't know my ownself. I also seen the Medicine Man fella who come to the village every once a while to talk to the folks there. Fact of the matter is that I spent the better part of that spring and into the summer there in that Indian village. Had no reason to move on, I guess.

Coupla times there was real nasty thunderstorms come through there, and I found out that I had no fear o' them anymore. I mean I did not go out there and try to get struck by lightnin' but I also did not get my brain muddled and get all quakey in the body when there was lightnin', even when it was real close.

After all them things that had happened to me or I guess done to me like bein' on top of that butte and sittin' in the little hut for two nights and all the stuff the Medicine Man teached me and the things the Chief Man done to me, after all of that, I found myself feelin' real peaceful like I have never felt before. It was like there was nothin' to get real upset about or get brain muddled about. 'Stead I could just sit and kinda watch the sun come up and watch them Indian folk doin' their work which now I sometimes often helped them with as much as I could. They had teached me a lot about their work and how to do it but I couldn't do it all 'cause some of it was real special or somethin'. Or they just didn't want me to know it! I even went back up that butte to the top one time and spent a whole night up there with no concern at all. When I come back down them Indian folk looked at me real nice like I was becomin' one 'o them.

One thing that had happened to me was real strange. Before I come to that Indian village I figured I was gettin' on in years and might not live to be much older 'though I was not what you would call old. Just that the way I had lived outdoors and walkin' a lot could cause a person to age real quick. Now I did not like the idea that I was goin' to die and in particular 'cause I had not seen everthin' that I had wanted to. There was places I still wanted to go like to the San Juan River which is what I started out to do before I got taken to this Indian village. I had heard from some folks about real interestin' things north of the Arizona Territory, and I had wanted to follow that Colorado River, the big one, up north to maybe where it had started out. But after bein' in that Indian village for most a year and a half I did not worry about that anymores. It was like I had a long time to live and should take my time to do what I wanted 'stead of walkin' too fast and maybe missin' some things along the way. Actual I felt like I might live for a very long time and maybe forever which was only a feelin' 'cause my brain knowed that ever human bein's got to die sometime. But that was the way I true felt.

One thing did seem a mite odd which was that there was times when I did not know if what I was seein' was really real. It was like what I was seein' was one o' them mirage things I had heard about and actual seen one time in the hot desert where you can see water clear as can be but when you come up to where you seen it it is not there. I could seem them buttes and the land between 'em and them scrub brush and other little plants and stuff but it seemed more like some picture a person had drawed and not the really real thing. I did not let that muddle my brain 'cause it seemed to be an all right kind of thing.

One thing that happens when you spend most of your life walkin' anywhere like in the Arizona Territory or anywhere else you spend a lot of time thinkin' about yourself and what you're goin' to do next and where you're goin' to go and how you're goin' to get yourself food and all that. In them past days I would be walkin' and thinkin' about how I'm kinda a little fella and maybe almost kinda ugly like that the Chief Man and how folks in the next tradin' post or town might find me when I walked in. Now I do not have them kinds of thinkin' anymore. I figure I am just my ownself and can't be anyone else so I'd better just go on without gettin' too concerned about how I look or how folks are goin' to find me when I walk in.

One other thing that had happened to me was that I sudden found out that I no longer wanted to go to the San Juan River as bad as I had wanted it before. Like I said before I still wanted to go there and to them other places like up the Colorado River but it didn't seem so needful anymore. It was like I could say to myself "That would be real nice, O'Leary, but if it don't happen it won't matter none."   I believe I also had less need for just goin' on walkin' all the time. Fact is I could not figure out why I had wanted to just keep on walkin' for all those years. It was not like them years was wasted 'cause I seen a lot and enjoyed most all of it. But it was also like there was some kinda fella inside of me that kept me goin' and now that fella had gone away, clear gone away and was no longer inside me.

As near as I can understand from bein' with the Medicine Man and that Chief fella, at least I thought he was a Chief, it seems them Indians thought that either I was a devil or a god when I walked past that shriveled little old man by the Big Black Rock. The had never seen anybody do that. Most folks, White Folks that is, usual turn away and went around the Big Black Rock which I didn't do. So they figured I was about to do them some harm or else bring them some good, and that's why they let me stay in that little hut and kept me up for those two nights and then put me on that butte for three days and had that young woman come to me, you know to be with me, and also had me stand in front of that changing woman. They figured if I was some kind of devil then all that would scare me, and I would up and leave or just go up in smoke or some such. And if it was a god then all kindsa good things would happen to them, and I would stay there and protect them from all kindsa evil. So it turned out I was just another human bein' except one that walked past the Big Black Rock instead of turnin' aside on my way to the San Juan River. That way they was happy I was not evil spirit but they was muddled in their brains and upset that I weren't no god.

What they did not know was that I had learneded a lot from those Indian folks. Only problem was I couldn't rightly tell them or tell you what is was I learneded. Main thing was that I learneded that sometime a muddled brain is a good thing if you can get it unmuddled, if there is such a word. And my brain was pretty unmuddled after all that time with them Indian folks.

# *How I Felt Pretty Good*

**As you may get from** what I have just told you, ma'm, I felt real good after spendin' that time in the Indian village and with them Indian folks. Fact is I had never felt no better in my entire life which is sayin' somethin'!

What I come to know after bein' away from the village and them Indian folks for a while, somethin' I will explain shortly about how I went away, was that my brain was able to see things in a whole new way. I could just see in my brain some ways in which people could live better 'though it was not real clear to me exact what those ways would be. I seen in the Indian village some troubles they had 'tween folks and when there was problems with growin' food or findin' animals to kill and butcher. In that way they was like all human beins'. But I kinda knowed that some of what they did was a real good way to live but that some other things they did was not so good. I never did figure out exact what the better way to live might be but was darned sure there was such a way and I tried for some time after I left that Indian village and them Indian folks to try to figure it out. I am still tryin' and will go on doin' that, ma'm.

Other thing is that I also knowed from that time with them Indian folks and all they put me through that somehow I was goin' to be able to do more right than wrong in my continuing life. Not that I had done a lot of bad, but I had never done a lot of good in any way. I had just kinda walked through the Arizona Territory without doin' much good or bad.

Now I somehow wanted to do more good, somethin' which I will continue to try.

I knew I was goin' to have to go back to my White man ways sooner or later. But I was goin' back with a dif'rent kinda way of thinkin' and doin'. Since I weren't afraid no more and my brain was not muddled, I could kinda see things more clear than I had before.

Now that made me feel real good inside. It was like when you eat real good food and that is cooked good and proper and served up in a real tasty way and you do not eat it too fast but take your time which is somethin' I only did occasional in my life up to this time. When food is cooked good and proper and served up tasty and you eat it just right then your insides feel real good and satisfied where if they ain't cooked good and is served up too salty or not salty enough and you eat it too fast then your insides feel just plain awful and sometimes you even gets pains in your gut. Well my insides felt real good from what I was teached and what I kinda learneded on my own during my time with the them Indian folks.

So I made up my unmuddled brain to go on with the rest of my ownself's life and try to do good to other folks but also to animals and such. Also I thought maybe I could do so by tellin' folks about my adventure and travel in that land with the Indian folks and the Indian village. That did not work out so well as I will tell you somewhat later.

# What Else I Come to Know from My Time in That Land

**Now as I said I** was feelin' good at this time, and now that I was away from that Indian village and them Indian folks I had come to contemplate what all had happened. I was teached that word 'contemplate' by a Priest Man back in the south of the Arizona Territory, and I liked the sound of it and it seemed like it fit what I was doin' at this time. That is, I was takin' time to think on everthin' that had happened without tryin' to make any sense of it. That's that's what the Priest Man had told men it was to contemplate. You think on things without tryin' to make sense of them. Other words you contemplate which is what I was doin'.

While in the middle of doin' that I come to see in my brain that first Big Black Rock and then that other one when I was comin' away from the Indian village and close to the San Juan River. I also remember what someone had told me about that third Big Black Rock which was to the northeast of the first one, and it seemed as though it would be pretty much straight east from the second one so's they made a big three-sided thing if you could get way up in the sky and look downward at the land.

Now I suspect there is more of them Indian folks and Indian villages in that area between them Big Black Rocks. There can't be too many 'cause there is not a lot of ways to get food or make food. Farmin' is kinda hard, and most of the farmin' I seen was at the bottom of them buttes where the water would run off after a rainstorm. There also ain't a lot of animals in there either 'cause they need grass and such to eat off of. The other problem is that they don't get a lot of rainstorms in that part of the Arizona Territory which you can understand 'cause it is desert. Otherwise there would be a lot of trees and grass and such.

So I come to believe that them Indian folks what lived in the spaces between them Big Black Rocks musta been a special kind of folk. They had a special way of livin' that would be hard for any White Man to understand. Even some of the folks that I heard about back East who live on earth that's hard to farm would not live long in the desert like these Indian folks.

Now it seemed to me that however they done it these Indian folks had some special kind of magic or somethin' that they used. I don't mean like castin' spells or anythin' like that. Nope I mean they had some special way of workin' the land and maybe talkin' to the sun and the clouds and such. I seen some of it with that Medicine Man who seemed like he knew ahead of time if there was goin' to be a rainstorm or if the wind was goin' to blow hard from some other way than it currently was.

I believe them Indian folks had somethin' that we White folk do not understand and prob'ly never will, and I sure do not know what it is even though I was in the middle of it for better part of a year. I sure know that bein' then somehow did somethin' to me and particular 'cause of all the things that Chief Man and the Changing Woman did to me and the Medicine Man showed me. It was a whole diff'rent way of livin' and workin'. I sure wish I did know what it was but all I can do is talk about what happened to me while I was there.

Now then I original thought them little men standin' by the Big Black Rocks was kinda guardians of this land but now I have changed my mind. I do believe it is the Big Black Rocks theirselves that is the guardians. The little Indian fellas just stand by the Big Black Rock Guardians.

If any person would ask me about that land inside the Big Black Rocks, I would tell them to stay away! They is some kind of signposts to tell strangers what is in there, and that is why them Big Black Rocks is so black and so high up out o' the ground and how they is so different from them red rock buttes and that brown sand all over. Them Big Black Rocks is unnatural and don't belong in the desert where they are at. There is somethin' special about that land and them Indian folks and anybody who'd stray in there had better be ready for some almighty strange things to happen. So it'd be better to just stay away.

# How I Went Away

**It seemed as though the** time had come for me to move on and try to get over to the San Juan River as I had original intended to do. However, I did find it somewhat hard to think about goin' away from that Indian village and the Chief Man and the Medicine Man and even the Changing Woman 'though I had only seen her a coupla time in the better part of a year or maybe more that I had spent with them. I did kinda lose track of what time of year it was except that it was hard to forget when the sun rose higher and higher in the sky and there was no rainstorms and not even many clouds all of which showed it was summer.

Now I had no idea how to tell them Indian folks that I was thinkin' about leavin' them. I had learned me some more Indian words but they was only good to talk about food or the weather or some such. So one day I went lookin' for the Chief Man which was not in his house that day. I kept lookin' and found him out by hisself sittin' next to one of them small bush-trees that grows in the desert. They don't give off much shade mainly 'cause they is so small and they is hard to get underneath. He nods to me, and I nod to me.

I sign that I would like to come over to him and talk which I do with my hands and then touch my lips like I was sayin' somethin'. The Chief Man motions me over, and I set next to him which I believe is a real honor 'cause I had never sat next to a chief before. After a brief while I start drawin' in the dirt a picture of me as I see myself. Well it was more one o' them stick figures like little childrens draw. Then I draw a picture of my little hut and a couple of the buttes around there. I also draw some other huts and houses so's to make it look like the Indian village. All the while the Chief Man is lookin' down at my pictures. It was like he thought they was actual interestin'.

Then I take the picture of me and draw my bedroll on the back of that figure, and I try to show the legs walkin' which is somewhat hard with a stick figure. I finally figure out to draw a couple o' them stick figures movin' away from the village, and I even figure out to make them stick figures get smaller.

That Chief Man then looks at me, and he motions with his one hand like he is pushin' someone away. I get the idea that he understands that I am wantin' to leave. He nods and gets up and walks back to his house.

Well that seemed real easy so then I had to figure out when I was goin' to actual leave the village. After some thinkin' I figure out to do it in two days. That gives me one day to walk around that Indian village and kinda say goodbye as best as I can. So the next day I do just that. I walk around, and it is like everybody knows that I am leavin'. Some of them Indian folks nod to me and even smile. Many of 'em make that same motion the Chief Man did which is a kinda pushin' thing at I nod to them. and smile as best I can 'cause now I am feelin' a little down in the spirits 'cause I will be goin' out on my own again walkin' the Arizona Territory.

On that second day after I had gone around the village I ate myself some breakfast and rolled up my bedroll. I come out of the little hut in which I had lived for the better part of a year or maybe more and there was the whole Indian village, I mean all of them Indian folks, standin' there to see me leave. Well I come near to sheddin' a tear or two 'cause I don't think anyone before had ever come to see me off. Usual I just walked away without no one knowin' anythin' about it or carin'. So I nod and smile to them and march right out of there as quick as can be to not show my real feelins'.

I walked on for most of a day with no sign of that San Juan River anywhere. I was headed almost straight north from the Indian village which I could do from the way the sun was shinin' and which way the buttes casted their shadows. When that old sun was direct over my head I knowed the shadows was anythin' straight south 'cause the sun would slide along in the more or less northern sky in the summer. So I just walked opposite from the shadows.

That evening I set up my camp in a wash where there was some cottonwood trees growin'. Them big old cottonwood trees was always my friends in my walkin' through the Arizona Territory 'cause they grow just about anywhere there is some water in a draw or wash or along a river. That night I slept just fine with no worries and just bein' able to imagine my ownself along the banks of the San Juan River right ahead.

In the mornin' I got up and I ate the last of the corn mush and beans them Indian ladies had give me, rolled up my bedroll, and started walkin' again. The whole day was spent in walkin' along leavin' them red buttes behind me. About this time I could just see some big white clouds way off in the northeast from where I was. Then there was another night I spent in my bedroll. This time I was able to find me a fine young rabbit which I was able to hit with a thing called a throw stick which is just a stick that is big enough to throw at a rabbit so as to either kill it or make it so it can't run away. Actual a throw stick must also be the right size, and it should be bent a little so's to make it spin round and round when you throws it. That young rabbit was almost dead when I got to it at which time I whacked it on the head. In a hour or a little more I was able to roast up the meat of that rabbit on a small fire I had made and had him for dinner. No more o' them beans and corn mush!

Next day I started up again, and in just a few miles I seen another one of them big black rocks ahead. It was kinda off to my right hand side so that's when I no longer went straight north but headed for that big black rock which kinda pulled me over to it. It did not look like that big black rock which I seen at the beginning of this story. This one was somewhat smaller I believe. Not as high up and more longish. It sure stood up there and made for a good mark for me to head to. Which, as I said, I did.

(*Editor's Note: This "big black rock" was probably what is now known as Alhambra Rock just a few miles southwest of Mexican Hat, Utah.*)

When you is walkin' all alone by yourself in the desert or mountains it is a good thing to have some kinda mark to show yourself where to go. That is why I started walkin' toward that big black rock. Now it is real hard to judge how far away anythin' is in the desert unless you knows how actual big it is. So I had no idea how far this thing was off over there.

Then I seen in the far off another damn, excuse me ma'm, dust devil startin' to whip up just like most a year afore over at that Big Black Rock. At this time I really ain't to interested in seein' another dust devil considerin' what happened the last time. Well that danged dust devil starts comin' right at me, and all I could think was that it would come over me and my brain would be all muddled again and some Indian folks would come get me and my whole story would start over again. So I just stands there total dumb and wait for it while I am sayin' some kinda prayer to God that I do not remember and it was one of the first times in my life I ever prayed about anything'. Then somethin' real strange happens. That dust devil comes over toward me and then kinda stops. Almost like it was lookin' at me! That made me pray whatever I was prayin' even more. That's when somethin' ever stranger happened. That dust devil musta seen somethin' about me 'cause it kinda slid over sideways and went right past me and into the desert which I watched until that thing just sorta blew itself up in the air and disappeared.

Once that dust devil did that dance around me and went off away, I kept on walkin' north or more like northwest towards that Big Black Rock which was still some miles away 'though it looked somewhat closer that it actual was. I can say that now 'cause it took me the better part of two days to get to the Big Black Rock 'cause there was a whole lot of canyons and arroyos between where I was and where the Big Black Rock was.

# What I Ran Into that Stopped Me

**It were a whole two** nights later that I final camped what I thought would be just a short way to the San Juan River which was my original place I wanted to be most of a year before. It had been a very strange year that I had spent with then Indian people. So I set up my little old camp right next to a small butte what stood up only maybe ten-twelve feet and was right next to a arroyo. By this time I had made some rabbit meat jerky only by strappin' strips o' that meat onto my bedroll and let it dry out in the sun and wind as I went on walkin'. It took most of a day to dry that meat out. It weren't real jerky 'cause jerky is made with salt to keep it all right, but in the desert you can just dry the meat out and it don't ever go bad. I had also been able to collect some plant leaves that I knowed was okay to eat. I had not had any corn mush, bean, and dried squash now for some days which was all right with me.

The next day I was ready to get over to the San Juan River and cross it into some land that was north of the Arizona Territory, at least that is what I thought, and to see some new things from what I had seen in the Arizona Territory. Now it is real hard to see where a river has cut a canyon in the desert 'cause all the land is so flat. Sometimes in walkin' you can be goin' along and sudden like there is a canyon or a arroyo right in front of you where you did not expect it. So I could not even guess how far away that San Juan River was from where I had spent the night.

Then it came up real fast. I could not hear the river which was a little strange 'cause normally when you is comin' up on a big river like the San

Juan River you can kinda hear the water, and I did not hear anythin'. When I got to the canyon I knew right away why I could not hear it! That canyon seemed about a thousand feet straight down on both sides with the San Juan River runnin' between them walls which was only maybe a couple hundred feet apart. That canyon was so deep and narrow that the San Juan River waters down below was in shadow where I stood. Fact is I believe that there was some parts of the San Juan River in that part where the sun did not shine but maybe ten-fifteen days a year and that would be in the middle of the summer time.

Now here I was where I had wanted to be, and there was no way I was goin' to get down to and across that San Juan River from where I was standin'. When I looked either direction from where I stood, that is to my right side or to my left side, that canyon was there but in a real strange way. The San Juan River and that canyon was looping back and forth like a damn snake, excuse the language, ma'm. They shoulda called it the Snakey River if this is the way it was all the way along. The twistin' o' that San Juan River was not like anythin' I had ever seen before. Some of them loops almost come back on theirselves so's if you was raftin' or canoein' that San Juan River right here you could start out goin' west and then find out you was headin' south and then goin' east and then you was goin' south again and then almost goin' west again.

*Editor's Note: O'Leary is here describing what is now known as the Goosenecks of the San Juan just southwest of Mexican Hat, Utah. There is a Utah state park from which a visitor can view the Goosenecks.*

Now I had take my brain and figure out which way to go from where I was. I could go east where it seemed maybe the land dropped a ways closer to the San Juan River. I mean the land got lower down and maybe there was a way to cross that San Juan River. I could go west which was kinda away from where I eventual wanted to be, at least so I thought. I had not knowed before I came to the San Juan River how awful big it real was. It was about the same as the Big Colorado River which I had left some time before, well I left it most of a year before so my memory of it might not have been total accurate.

What that snakey part of the San Juan River did to me was to make me stop right there and do some thinkin'. When there is somethin' blockin' the way you want to go sometime it just makes you stop and do some thinkin' which is what I did. This same thing had happen to me a few times before like when I got to the Little Colorado River Canyon across which the only to go was to fly where I had come to it. And the same thing with the Big

Colorado River Canyon which was even wider and deeper than the Little Colorado River Canyon. Both times I had to stop right there in my own tracks and do some thinkin' mostly about where to go but sometime also about whether I should go on or not.

Both them times by the Little Colorado River Canyon and also the Big Colorado River Canyon I set myself up a camp. At that Little Colorado River Canyon there was not much in the way of wood or nothin' what I could build with so I just clumped some rocks and dirt together and made a kinda three-sided shelter. I was able to find enough scrub brush to make a kinda roof on the thing which allowed my some shade durin' the day and might of kept off the rain if it had rained. But it never did. At the Big Colorado River Canyon there was a lot more trees and such, and I built myself a right tidy little hut out of whatever wood I could find layin' around since I did not have a hatchet or axe what I could use to cut anythin' down. I stayed in that little hut for most of two weeks I believe 'cause it was somewhat real interestin' to look into that great big canyon and to see all the sights there was to see. One thing I found there was that there was somewhat too much to see, and I could not understand the whole thing at once. The Little Colorado River Canyon was not as interestin' but it was a bit more frightenin' in that the walls of that canyon went straight down. I figured at the Big Colorado River Canyon if I was to fall off the edge there would be trees and shrubs and such to stop me. At least so I hoped.

So I figured to do the same and build me some kinda shelter there at the San Juan River Canyon in the snakey part of the San Juan River. Only problem was there weren't much in the way of anythin' to make a shelter. I final found some rocks and a place in the dirt which was kinda sunk in and made my ownself a little shelter which was not much good and only made shade for a small part of the day.

# How I Didn't Want to Go

**This part of my story** seems real strange to me after all I had went through with them Indians. Here I was at the San Juan River which is where I wanted to be all the time. I had come to that snakey part of the river but soon understood that there was places where I could cross it upstream if I wanted. That was the part that muddled my brain again. Found out I didn't want to cross that river. What I really wanted was to go back to them Indian folks even though there was no way I could talk to them or understand them. But I figured that after some time I could learn their language and be part of their village. That had a real powerful pull on me.

I had felt real good with that Changing Woman even though I cried when she touched me on the shoulders and never did really try to comfort me like my Mama would. And I remembered how good I felt when I come to realize what had gone on and what had happened to me. I remembered how my mind was no longer muddled but very straight and understandin'. Shoot why wouldn't I want to go back?

Them people treated me real good in some ways although it didn't always appear that way when I was goin' through all that stuff they made me do. Like the time that young woman come to me and wanted to be with me but I ran away from her. That was good, that I ran away, but it was bad because I did really want to be with her.

I knowed that when I got back with my own White Folks that my brain would get all muddled up again and things would get real complicated like they always do. Meanwhile when I lived with them Indian folks I found it to be real peaceful and nice. Sure their lives was hard in the way of gettin' food and makin' sure they had water and they had some troubles among themselves. But who's life ain't? Their trouble seemed a good deal smaller that most of the ones I seen in White Folks villages and towns. These Indians didn't go around tryin' to kill each other like in some White folk towns I been in. And they didn't curse at one another, either. Also they didn't get drunk and do stupid things after drinkin'. Maybe I just seen part of the way they lived, but I think I seen most of it.

So I was sittin' there lookin' at that snakey part of the San Juan River which is where I had wanted to be, but now that I was there I weren't so sure anymore. I got to thinkin' back on that Indian village and them Indian folks and the Medicine Man and the Chief Man, and it seemed pretty darn nice back there. They done real right by me what with feedin' me even when there weren't much in the way of rations. I must say, ma'm, that eatin' nothin' but corn mush, beans, and dried up squash with some rabbit meat ever once in a while was not the best part. I have ate better on my own out in the desert and in the mountains. But them Indian folks was real nice to me even when they hanged me over the edge of that butte and made me stay awake for two nights without no sleep. Lookin' back on all that it weren't as bad as it seemed at the time.

My brain had been mostly unmuddled by the end of my stay in that Indian village and with them Indian folks. Now I was right afraid of gettin' my brain all muddled up again as I have said before. So I was sittin' not sure if I should go on back to my little hut and try to learn more of them Indian words and maybe become a kinda Indian which didn't seem too likely. Or I could try to figure out how to get across that darn snakey San Juan River which set right in front of me by goin' upstream a ways.

I have knowed some time before that there are times when you go through some hard times and then after you think back on it and it weren't so bad. Now lookin' back I weren't even sure that my time in the Indian village with them Indian folks was all that bad. There was some times when I were somewhat scared, I must tell you, particular when I was bein' hung over the edge of that butte! But most of them it was somewhat good or somewhat not either good or bad. Just kinda level which is not a bad way to live out a person's life.

So I sat there and thunk about the whole thing real hard and could not come to a way to go which was either back or on across the San Juan River. My brain was not really muddled, I do believe, 'cause I could see quite clear the two things that I could do, and they both seemed equal good with not either one bein' much better than the other. Well I final decided to go back to that Indian village with them Indian folks. Figured I would live out my life there doin' some kinda good with them Indian folks.

# *What Come to Get Me*

**Sometime things just do not** work out like you had planned them 'cause I was ready to go back to that Indian village and them Indian folks when one more o' them strange things happened to me. I had rolled up my bedroll and walked away from that little shelter I had made for my ownself out of rocks and some dirt and sand. The direction I went off to was the opposite of the one I had come to the place on so I figured it would get me back to them Indian folks and that Indian village. I could also see that Big Black Rock ahead o' me and a little to my right hand side.

I had not walked more than ten-twelve yards than a big old raven comes flappin' his wings right around my head so's I had to stop to protect myself from that bird. Well he don't exactly stop. What he does is sit down right in front of me to where I would have to take my next step.

I never did like them ravens 'cause they is so black and their eyes is black and if you ever seen on up close they also got a big mouth-bill with which to peck on things. Also they is known to mostly east dead animals layin' in the desert although I suspect sometimes them ravens also each seeds or nuts and such. I just don't like critters that eat dead stuff which is also true of vultures and eagles. I do like some hawks 'cause they fly around 'til they seem somethin' alive that they want to eat and swoop down on it. I seen them swoop down like that and pick up a whole prairie dog and fly off with it!

So this raven sits right in front of me to where I cannot move toward where I want to go. Ain't no raven goin' to stop me so I step to one side in order to get around him, but he just hops over the same way. Well now this ain't good. I step to the other side, and that raven hops over that way. No way is he goin' to let me walk in the direction I want to go.

Other thing that bothered me about that raven when I got to thinkin' about it with my unmuddled brain was that he was the exact same color as them Big Black Rocks 'cept he was a big black bird. 'Course he weren't as big as the Big Black Rocks.

Next thing I know that big black raven lifts 'most straight up off the ground and 'most right in my face which sure scared me a bit 'though I knowed that big black raven could not kill me or nothin'. He sure was bein' mean.

Well I turned me around and started walkin' back to the San Juan River where I had camped out for some time only ten-twelve yards back from where that big black raven stopped me. That sure seemed to please that big black raven 'cause he lifts up into the air 'bout six-seven feet in front of me and starts flyin' the direction of the San Juan River. At this time I did not want to fight with that big black raven no more so I followed him for a while figurin' I could turn around and head the way I wanted when he was not lookin'.

Problem is that big black raven never did stop lookin'. He just kept on flyin' around in front of my ownself and off to the edge of the San Juan River canyon where the San Juan River was so snakey as I have told you before. When we come close to the edge of the canyon that big black raven turns himself to the east and just start sqwakin' and hollerin' the way ravens with do. That's when I turned back to go the way I wanted 'cause the big black raven was some yards ahead of me. Minute I turned he was right back in my face, and then set down right in front of me. No way was I goin' to go back to them Indian folks and that Indian village with big black raven all around me.

That's when I walked a bit and found a stick which I was goin' to use to shoo that big black raven away. Well I might as well have tried to shoo a elephant or a alligator away pictures of which I had seen in a book one time. That raven would not be shooed away. It just kept flyin' at me and then away and then at me again.

I final gave up and kept walkin' east along the San Juan River. That old big black raven kept right up with me the whole day and would not let me stray from my path along the San Juan River. As we went along the sides of the San Juan River canyon got lower down, and it was no longer snakey. Just the normal twists and turns of a big river.

It got to be evenin' so I stopped and that big black raven stopped right at the same place 'cept now we was more down along the river edge and that big black raven perched hisself on a cottonwood tree limb while I made myself a bed. I was still thinkin' I might be able to sneak away from that big black raven, but there was no such luck. I sure found out that ravens do not sleep at all. They just set and watch.

So as it turns out that big black raven never did let me go back to them Indian folks and that Indian village. 'Stead it led me right to a small settlement on the banks of the San Juan River where there was some twenty-thirty people, mostly men, who did tradin' and such. For the next several months which was the rest of the summer and early fall I walked around that land along the San Juan River. I never did go back to them Indian folks and that Indian village.

# My Troubles After I Left

**So there I was in** that part of the country that was north of the Arizona Territory and which was no yet settled much 'though there was a camp or two along the San Juan River for folks to trade with the Indians in that part of the country. These camps was small and could not rightly be called Tradin' Posts for they did not have all the things you would find in a Tradin' Post. 'Stead they were mostly four-five small houses with mostly men occupyin' them. What they did in these small camps was some farmin' right along the San Juan River banks and a little ways away, and they did some huntin' in the rock hills around them.

This was not the interestin' country I had thought to come to so I started walkin' again back down in the direction of the Arizona Territory. What I had come to see was somethin' folks had told me was big mountains that was so big they usual had snow on 'em until well into the summer months so they was topped off with white which would have been right nice to see. I found out that where those mountains was some long miles from where I was. So that's why I decided to go back to the Arizona Territory.

'Though I had wanted to come to the San Juan River now that I was there it didn't seem all that good to me. Normal I woulda been downcast and maybe muddled by findin' out I didn't want to be where I though I had wanted to be. With my learnins' from those Indian folks there weren't any muddle in my brain at all about this. I just did not want to be there anymore.

I started my walkin' again. While I did that I kept thinkin' about that Indian village and them Indian folks but now I knowed I could not go back. I was a White Man and would not have even been a Indian in any way at all.

Durin' my walkin' I did come across various White Folks which I would want to say was like me but they wasn't! They had white skin all right, but they was way different from me. One of them things that showed me they was different was in the way they talked. When I come back to the places where there was White people I soon found out that they talked a lot louder than the Indian folks in that Indian village and louder even than me. I never was much for talkin' anyways, and now I did not talk anymore than I ever did but when I did talk it was nice and easy, kinda slow and quiet 'though I tried not to whisper which would sound like you was tryin' to tell only a secret. Now the White Folks did not holler, but they talked real fast as far I could tell and they talked loud like everone was almost deaf. At least that how it sounded to me.

Was the same way when they was walkin' or workin' or whatever. They was all in some kinda hurry to get things done so's they could go on and do more somewhere else. That seem kinda foolish to me. I learned with them Indian folks in that Indian village that the best way is to work slow and deliberate and get everthin' right and do only as much as you can do and don't try to do no more. Them Indian folks in that Indian village woulda never gone on tryin' to keep diggin' up the ground or plantin' or harvestin' or buildin' a house when it were late in the day and they was tired. They knew 'nough to stop when they was tired. Now it seemed like most of the White people I met or seen kept on workin' when they was tired and that made them real tetchy and then they begun talkin' nasty to one another. Sometimes they'd even talk nasty to me 'though I had done nothin' but walk up to their town or settlement.

At one of them small towns in the Arizona Territory I stayed for most of a week 'cause I had made a blister on my one foot and did not want to make it any worser. I had done that once, that is kept on walkin' with a blister, and it had become real bad painful and full of pus and all. That time I had to stop walkin' for most of three weeks to let that thing heal up real good. So now I knowed better. Anyway I was stayin' in this town which I must tell you was just sleepin' in my bedroll in one of the stalls in the livery place in that town. They did not ask me to pay for that, and I tried to help out as best I could with chores around the livery to pay for my keep. The owner was real nice, and he even brought me food from his own table 'though I believe what he brought was what them at the table did not want or did not finish up. Well he was a nice enough man not too young but not yet old neither, and he was married to this younger woman who would come and talk to me at times durin' the day. I told her about my walkin' the Arizona Territory, and she liked to hear about that. I tried tellin' her about my time in the Indian village with them Indian folks, but that did not interest her as much. She told me that she had always wanted to go adventurin' but of course was married and could not do that. She come to the stables most every day and wanted to hear of the mountains I had seen and the kinds of plants they had in the desert down south in the Arizona Territory.

'Course I was willin' to talk about them things 'cause they was interestin' to me as well. Her husband, the nice man, had to go on to a nearby town to do some horse tradin' and was gone for two-three nights. Well one of them nights this married lady come to the stables long after dark and right to my stall where I was layin' in my bedroll almost fully sleepin'. She lays down right next to me which I did not want nor expect. But she did. Then she starts sweet talkin' to me, and I knowed what she wanted which I would not do. First off I liked her nice husband who had been good to me, and second I was no longer real interested in layin' with a woman as I have explained to you before, ma'm. This made her real upset, and she begun slappin' me and talkin' mean. Then she up and went back to her house. When her husband came back she told him that I had tried to lay with her, but he for some reason did not believe her 'cause I believe that she had tried to do that same thing before with other men. I stayed in that stable and stall for another week and then left that town.

I did not particular like this world what I had come back to with the loud talkin' people and people what was all excited and gettin' all riled up and people what did not even believe any of my story. That begun to get my brain all muddled up again just like before I went and stayed with those Indian folks in that Indian village. Only way I could get my brain unmuddled again was to get away from folks for a while, that's them White Folks, and go off and watch the clouds and see which way the sun was shinin' on the ground and then remember about hangin' from my heels over the edge of that butte but was not dropped. Then my brain begun to get unmuddled, and I could go on walkin' the Arizona Territory again.

Result of all that excitement of White Folks and their loud talkin' and all is that my walkin' seemed to take a real long time. Some days I felt like I had been walkin' for a hundred years or more while that time in the Indian village with them Indian folks seemed like it only took about two weeks when in fact I was there with them for most of a year and some months. At times it seemed like it should be the other way 'round. Livin' in that Indian village with them Indian folks was so light and easy that time shoulda seemed like it was passin' real slow, but it did not.

It do seem sad that what them Indian folks in that Indian village had found out about the ground and the sky and the clouds and all could not be learneded by the White people. I believe that everone could live a lot easier if they all learneded about that kind of thing instead of about wars and killin' and makin' great amounts of money and gettin' more and more land that they can bare use. Seems like in some ways the Indians folks in that Indian village and maybe all folks what don't have much actual gets along better than the folks who has a lot and are always wantin' to get more.

What muddled my brain more 'en anythin' was how people took it when I tried to tell my story. I would start out with the Big Black Rock and the dust devil and sometime they would already start laughin' at me like I was tellin' some kinda fairy tale like what my dear Mama had told me sometimes. If they would not be laughin' but listen some more then they would start shakin' their head when I told 'em about the Medicine Man and the way the Chief Man done to me. They did not believe a word of any of it. I did not even try to tell them about Changin' Woman or the young woman who come to me. They sure would not have believed anything about what came to get me, that raven, when I was done with the Indian village and them Indian folks and on my way to the San Juan River. No ma'm, they would not believe a word of that. So I had to keep walkin' without talkin' and keep my story to my ownself.

Maybe my tellin' you this story, ma'm, and you writin' it down will be one way that other folks could learn from what I learneded from those Indian folks who live beyond them black rocks which as I have said I now consider to be guardians of that land. I think I am going to go back there and live among'st them people. Maybe I could live behind them guardians and feel a whole lot better. Don't care if no raven tries to turn me back or not.

# The Ending of My Story

**Well that is about all** I can recollect, ma'm, about my story. Some folks will think it is a bunch of hooey, and that is okay with me. They can believe my story or not. I knows what did happen, and what I have told you is most of the story. What I mean is all that I could recollect.